TWISTED

From the Pen of

Ni'cola

*Michelle
Keep the
pages
flipping
Ni'cole*

NCM PUBLISHING

www.ncmpublishing.com

Published by NCM Publishing

Library of Congress Catalog Card No: 2011902335
ISBN: 978-0-9833461-1-1

Twisted:
Written by: Ni'cola Mitchell
Edited by: Leila Jefferson
Publicist: Kolanda Scott
Text Formation: Write On Promotions
Cover:
        Design and Layout: The Cover Studio
        Model: Sharonna Shelton
        Stylist: Haute Thrifture
        Make-up Artist: Candace Lock Johnson

Published by
NCM Publishing
Las Vegas, NV 89108
www.ncmpublishing.com

Dedication

This novel is dedicated to my sister Janet Marcia Morris-Smith. I have been so lost since you have been gone. Girl, I love you so much, and I promise that I will continue to make you proud. You have always been my inspiration...

Thank you for the angels that you have left to watch over me as well so NeNe, Shardai, Dricie, and KO this book is dedicated to you too.

TWISTED

A Woman Scorned......

I removed my Armani Exchange sunglasses and extended my left hand to take a good look at my ring finger. I was in love with my two carat, sky blue diamond, platinum engagement ring Dale gave me when he proposed to me.

The ring that he had given me just hours before I went on a high speed chase with a damn near empty gas tank through the city of North Las Vegas, chasing him and his chick of the moment. The *same* ring that he had given me before he knew that Ashley, his mistress from the garage, was pregnant. The *same* ring that he had given me despite of the secret love affair I discovered that him and Eva, my supposedly best friend, was entangled in.

Yea, I was oh *so* in love with the beautiful ring that I did not think twice as I stood in line at the small pawnbroker downtown to do the inevitable.

I was about to pawn it. That's right. I walked up to the elderly Middle Eastern woman that stood behind the counter and asked her for her best offer.

The lady peered at me over her wire reading glasses for a moment before stepping away to speak to her supervisor. I really was not in the mood for speculations and I glared right back at her, my hazel colored eyes never blinking.

I knew that we were in Las Vegas, home of big dreams and huge losses. The land of gambling your rent money away and spending all night at the neighborhood casino trying to flip it back. The city known for its connection of sin and the motto of by any means necessary; but my situation was not the case.

I was far from being hard up for money. I did not harbor any typical addictions such as gambling, drinking, sex, or smoking. I did not have to live by the rules of robbing Peter to pay Paul.

My kryptonite was on a totally different level. My addiction was Dale and the heartbreak that he proposed on me on so many occasions. Getting rid of the ring was going to be the first step of my road to recovery, and I really didn't care about what that old lady nor anyone felt or thought about what I was doing.

Pawning the ring was in the *best interest of me.*

Back to Reality

Dionni

"Dionni Stone." An unfamiliar male voice came across my line. Glancing at my cell-phone, I was shocked that it was three thirty-six in the morning.

Damn, this better be important," I thought as I tried to get myself together.

"Yes, this is she," I replied in barely a whisper. Releasing a yawn, I rolled over, pulling the blanket over my head. "How may I help you?"

I rarely received calls from unknown numbers and usually sent those calls straight to voicemail, but after the fifth round of rings, I knew that something wasn't right.

"This is Officer Franklin from the North Las Vegas Police Department and you were listed as a next of kin for a Ms. Tiana Jones."

Tiana!

Hearing her name made the hairs stand up on the back of my neck. I sat up in the bed, instantly becoming alert. Since the day I caught Eva and Dale getting it in, I had been in New York at my Aunt's hiding out. I knew that it had been a moment since I had spoken with T, but I tried to at least send her a text message every day. Why the hell was "North Town" calling me?

"Okay, is something wrong?" I asked, taking in a slow breath.

All kinds of things were flowing through my mind as I waited for the officer to explain himself. Besides her boyfriend Antwan, Tiana didn't have any immediate family. Since college, Eva and I had been all that she has had. *Eva.* Just the thought of her made me cringe. Shaking my head, I tried to clear my thoughts and digest everything the officer tried to tell me.

"Tiana was found raped and beaten inside of her house by a neighbor. Her front door was wide open for at least an hour and the neighbors became suspicious and called us. Currently, she is a coma and has been admitted into University Medical Center, one of the best trauma units in Las Vegas. I think it would be in your best interest to get to the hospital as soon as possible."

In a coma? What the hell happened? Who would want to hurt her?

Tears began to stream down my face as I started to search for paper. I tried to stay calm as I grabbed a pen and jotted down the hospital's intensive care information from the officer.

"Officer Franklin," I began. "Do you think that she is going to make it? I am not in town right now, but I am going to get back as soon as possible. Do I have enough time..." A slight gasp released from my throat as I felt myself beginning to hyperventilate.

"Ms. Stone, this is all the information that I can give you right now, but I do suggest that you hurry and get here. I do have one more question for you, and then I am going to let you prepare for your return. What can you tell me about Antwan, her boyfriend? The neighbors informed us that they live together.

We found his name in her cell phone and have been trying to reach him all night, but his phone is going straight to voicemail. As of right now, he is a suspect until we find out otherwise. So, if you see or speak to him before we find him; let him know that he is wanted for questioning."

My heart skipped a beat. *Antwan!* The thought of that fool did not even cross my mind till he mentioned his name.

"Officer Franklin," I began slowly. "I hope he does not have anything to do with what happened to Tiana, but I can assure you one thing, if he does, I promise, you will be the first to know. As soon as I hang up, I am going to try to call him myself."

We said our goodbyes, and I hurried and called my travel agent. I knew it was too early to be calling her, but I needed her to expedite my return trip to Vegas.

What is really going on?

Dale

Ding dong, ding dong, and ding dong. The sound of my doorbell interrupted the peaceful slumber that I was partaking. It was the first time in a while that I had slept throughout the night since the baby had been born, and I was trying to make the best of it. I glanced at the alarm clock and tried to focus on the numbers that were displayed. 6:29?! Who the hell was bold enough to be at my door at that time of the morning?

The ringing intensified, followed by hard knocks. I placed the pillow over my face and tried to go back to sleep, but the persistent person on the other end of my front door was beginning to play melodies with my bell. I hopped up out the bed and pulled on my boxers that were sprawled across the floor.

This better not be Ashley with any bullshit! I thought as I hurried to the front door. Since the birth of Raven, Ashley had been going nonstop. I really thought she believed if she stressed my nerves enough I would finally give, and allow her and the baby to move me.

Granted, I was not happy with the circumstances that my daughter was conceived, but I was not a complete asshole, either. I mean, I did have my doubts, but just like any man questioning the paternity of their child, I had Raven tested as soon as her grandmother cut her umbilical cord.

I always wanted a daughter and for the last several years, I was convinced that the only woman that was going to be the mother of my child was Dionni. But, like that great book entitled The Bible stated, *The only person that has the final say is God,* so that was how my life was changed overnight.

Now Ashley believed that she had a pass to pop up at my house any time she pleased in the name of Raven, but I had some news for her. It would be the *last* time that that crazy ass chick was going to find her way to 6120 Berrien Springs St.!

Without even asking who it was, I swung the door open, pointing my left index finger in her face.

"What the fu..."

Before I could finish, my brother, Antwan, pushed past me and slammed the door shut behind him. "Dale, before you start tripping, let me speak my peace!" Antwan asked, pacing back and forth between the window and the front door. "That shit is locked, right?" he asked, playing with my front while checking the deadbolt. "Dude, I am sorry barging in your crib in the middle of the night like this. Is Candy here?" he asked, finally calming down and giving the room a once over.

"Yea, Twan, and she are sleep, so you need to watch your tone and tell me what is going on."

My brother used to live with me, but for the past year he and Tiana, Dionni's best friend, had been living together in a nice townhouse in Mountain's Edge. Any other time he would have had full access to the spot, but since the night that I got caught having the best ménage a trios that a man could have by him and Tiana, I had to act like my house was Fort Knox, and put a password on everything and change up the locks.

"Mmmaaannnn, D," Antwan said with a look of absolute fear on his face. "I done fucked up!"

"Twan, it's late and I am tired. I just got home from watching Raven and I am tired, man. If you and Tiana are tripping, you can chill out here, man. Go crash in your old room and let's discuss this in the morning. "Aright?"

I brushed past Twan and headed back to my room. I really was not in the mood to be having any heart to heart conversations on how Tiana cussed him out for fucking off her money again. He had a gambling problem or something, because lately he was blowing money, but then flipping it back at record speeds.

"Dale, this doesn't have to do with Tiana. *Yet,* that is," Antwan mumbled under his breath.

I stopped and turned back to face my brother. "It don't?" I repeated, now confused as hell. "What does it got to do with then, 'Twan, and what do you mean by yet?"

So much bull shit began to run through my head as I waited for my brother to respond. He was only three years younger than me, but sometimes I felt like there was a decade between us.

His decision making techniques were not the greatest, but hell, neither were mine.

"Well, you know T wants to get married and have kids, right? So, I started going down on Boulder Highway and playing blackjack, and now I am all caught up."

Tears began to roll down my brother's face as a look of defeat crept across it. I didn't know what was going on, but at the looks of things I was not going to be getting any sleep.

"Man, chill out and tell me what's wrong. We are going to figure this out together, okay? Let's go into the game room, though, and talk. Like I said before, Candy is trying to sleep."

I followed Twan down the second flight of stairs that led to my game room that we entitled "The Dungeon."

Las Vegas, My Home

Dionni

Usually I slept like a baby on red eye flights, but this time it was different. Every time I closed my eyes, visions of Tiana lying in a hospital bed played over and over in my mind. I was trying to stay positive, but it was so hard.

Tiana was more than my friend; she was my sister. We went so far back. We had been friends since college and I didn't know what would happen to me if I lost her, but I if I lost her to some bullshit that Antwan had gotten himself mixed up in... Man!

I was trying so hard to not allow my mind to think like that. But, it was only human nature for me to wonder if that wonder that fool had something to do with this first.

Back in the day, Antwan did his share of dirt out in the street, but since he got back into the relationship with Tiana, I thought he had changed his colors. But, the situation just didn't seem right.

No one even knew that I was going to be back in town because I left so quickly. After I finalized my travel arrangements, I explained to my Aunt Leioni what was going on while I packed.

My Aunt listened in silence with her eyes closed and head bowed as I spoke. I knew that she was praying for Tiana's recovery. Once her eyes opened, tears dripped from her face. I thanked her for allowing me to stay there and getting my mind right before I stepped back into the real world.

My Aunt Leioni was the one that brought me to the realization that running from my past was only going to hinder my future if I wanted to move on with my life. She knew the whole story of what happened from Dale, then Zay and Eva, and never once did she judge me. She had only shown me the unconditional love that I needed.

The story of Dale.... Ugh... Everytime I thought about it I cringed. I have had so many night mares behind Dale.

The projection of the captain's voice coming from the overhead PA system interrupted my thoughts as he informed us of the temperature and time in Las Vegas.

A chill ran down my spine as I let out a deep breath. "Home sweet home," I whispered under my breath, gathering my items, and getting ready for departure.

Gasping for Air

Eva

"David, did she wake up yet?" I asked, gripping on the steering wheel. I had been sitting in the parking garage at UMC for forty-five minutes.

"No, boo, where are you? I am about to go home and lay down for a couple of hours. Dionni is not here if that is what you are worried about."

"Okay, David, I am almost there. Thank you for telling me what happened to her. I will talk to you later."

David and I bid each other goodbye, and I hung up.

The last time that I had seen Tiana we were not on the best of terms. She told me that Dionni left town, but not before she informed her of my relationship with Dale.

Every time I thought about that crazy ass night I felt sick. You see, Dale had been in an on and off relationship with Dionni for some years now and I knew that.

Shit, I was the one who introduced them. But, the coldest element to that equation was that I had been in a relationship with him just as long.

I knew that things were getting too close for comfort, but Dale had my mind and body so sprung that I could not see clearly.

In the beginning it was supposed to just be fun, but we both got caught up. Well, let me rephrase that, I got caught up. He just liked the fact that I did whateva he said.

We had too many close calls.

We were so sloppy.

But, did that stop me from going back for more?

Nope. I continued going and going.

Damn, I am such an idiot! I thought, shaking my head and thinking about the time Tiana caught us having sex with Nia, the girl that eventually took Dionni on a high speed chase. Yep, a threesome. And, for what? I didn't even like girls, but I let that man talk me into it. I just knew that she identified me because I looked right at her, but I guess it was too dark down there.

That night was so damn crazy! I didn't even know how Nia ended up joining us that night. Dale and I were lying on the couch in his game room. It was his birthday and I knew that Dionni was planning on taking him to Mexico the next day. I had Macaroni Grill cater our dinner from the appetizers to the wine selection. I had just sang him Happy Birthday, and was feeding him some gelato and watching the Biggie Smalls' *Notorious* movie when his phone rang.

Whenever I was there, he never had the phone volume up, let alone answer it so the sound startled me. He nudged me to get up while whispering into the phone.

It must have been Dionni, but it was still pissing me off. I was getting tired of playing second to her. It felt like an eternity passed before I heard him come back down, but he didn't emerge alone.

Following in pursuit carrying a plate of the food that *I* paid for was a small, light skinned girl whose hair flowed down almost to her waistline. I sat in disbelief as he introduced me to "Nia." She only nodded because her mouth was full of pasta.

I gave her a once over as she came closer to me. I had to admit that she was cute, but she you could tell that she was young, dumb, and full of cum. She wore a dress that barely covered her ass, and flip flops.

So many emotions were running through me as Dale smiled at me. I knew that Dale got down with other folks, but to let her come in while I was there let me know that Dale truly thought I was a joke.

"Nia came over here to tell me happy birthday, too. Aren't I the lucky one?" he said and bent down to kiss me.

"What the fuck!" Nia exclaimed, dropping her plate of food.

Damn, she took the words right out of my mouth, I thought.

I didn't think neither one of us were ready for his next move because she had the same look of confusion in her eyes as he planted a sensual kiss on to her lips as well, rubbing the outlines of my breasts through my shirt at the same time.

"Shhh," Dale whispered to her, separating her legs with his other.

"You like it when Daddy does this, right?" he continued to whisper between kisses.

I stood there frozen in my spot, not liking that I felt the wetness emerge between my legs.

The way that her body reacted to his touch was so sexy. She wrapped her arms around his neck and squatted in her stance, allowing him more access to her prized jewel.

It was obvious that Nia was turning Dale on, too, because he stopped rubbing my breasts and placed his other hand onto the small of her back, holding her in place.

I didn't know what came over me, but it felt as if I was having an outer body experience. Quickly, I shed my clothes and stepped closer to the pair.

Taking in a deep breath, I stepped behind Dale and pressed my body against his back. I wrapped my arms around his waist and unbuckled his pants.

"Ummm," he moaned out, finally breaking their kiss.

Nia's eyes slowly opened and she

looked me dead into the eyes. I could see that she was scared as well, but the control that Dale had over us was apparent to both of us.

Nia softly caressed my face with her right hand while caressing my breast with her left.

Dale ducked down and removed himself from between us. He turned off the movie, turned on some music, and removed his own clothes. After that, everything went in a blur. The next thing I knew, we were all naked and performing sexual favors to each other.

Dale commanded us to kiss, suck, and touch, and like puppets, both of us obliged in silence.

That was how we ended up riding Dale, Nia his mouth and me his dick, when Tiana snuck down the stairway and caught us.

The crazy thing about it was that I

knew I heard Tiana calling Dale, but I didn't say anything to alert my partners. Part of me wanted to get caught and stop harboring the secret. My heart pounded as I watched her come down the stairs.

I pulled Nia's head closer and began kissing her in an intense manner. My heart beat so fast. I opened my eyes and glanced at her again. That time, she was not alone. Antwan stood behind her, watching her reaction as well. I knew that it was going to go down.

Well, I thought it was.

Tiana was usually so strong and confrontational, but not in that circumstance. There was so much moaning and groaning going on that it must have overwhelmed her. I watched her grip the staircase and quickly back right into Antwan. I watched him grip her shoulders and whisper something to her.

Once she was gone, Antwan yelled

Dale's name, startling all of us. I could still see the look of confusion on Antwan's face once he realized that I was the third piece in the puzzle. He knew that Dale was fucking Nia, but we were pretty good at disguising our relationship.

Opening the car door, I tried to get rid of all thoughts of that night. It was not the time or the place. Tiana was lying up in some hospital bed in a coma and I was there loathing in my guilt.

Shaking my head, I hurried into the hospital.

Restless

Dionni

Oh my gosh, my back is killing me. I spent the night with Tiana, sleeping alongside her hospital bed in a very uncomfortable chair that gave you the illusion that it was going to recline, but really played with your emotions because it didn't.

When I first got there, I wasn't prepared to see her like that. She looked the same, but swollen. Even with the puffiness you could tell that T had lost a lot of weight.

I had been wracking my brain all night trying to figure out what was going on. The nurse informed me that she had been having visitors come and go all day, and that I just missed a female that I favored a couple of minutes before I arrived. My initial thought was that it must have been Eva because everyone always mistook us for sisters. My blood began to boil. I had to take a couple of deep breaths and shake those thoughts off. It was not the time to trip out on her. Even though she was trifling as hell, it didn't mean that she didn't love T.

But did she really have love for T? Did she love anyone besides herself? I know it is not my place to question her love, but Damn. I do.

I thought she was my best friend. Hell, we were best friends way before Tiana even *came* into the equation.

I have had so many restless and sleepless nights dreaming about Eva, and her ultimate betrayal. You see, it went down like this.

I pulled up to Dale's house and sat for a moment trying to get myself under control. I haven't spoken too or seen him since the high speed chase. I was devasted that I just found out that Ashley was pregnant.

I knew there was always a possibility that Dale had kids out in the world, but damn. To actually have the pregnancy confirmed...I was numb especially after loosing mine. Just the thought made me queasy all over again.

Dale's car was outside but when I tried to call him, but his phone went straight to voicemail. I got out of my car and walked to the door.

A feeling of déjà vu came over me. The hairs on my arms and the back of my neck rose. Shaking it off, I rang the doorbell and waited. No one answered.

Reaching in to knock on the door, I realized that the door was not all the way closed

I sat out there for a couple of more moments contemplating if I should go in or not. I rang the bell again. Still no response. Finally, I got the nerve together to go inside.

"Dale." I called out as I headed down the stairs to the game room. Something was not right. A cold chill ran through my body.

When I reached the bottom of the stairs, I called his name again. No one was there though, so I let out a sigh of relief.

It wasn't until I came back up the stairs when I finally heard a noise. It sounded like a slight moan. I stopped dead in my tracks. I called out Dale's name again, but there was still no response.

Something told me to leave, but I I had another feeling in the pit of my stomach telling me that I needed to stay and walk my tail down the hallway to his room.

The closer I got to the door, the louder the moans became. I knew that fool was there, but I just needed to see if he was there alone.

Slowly I turned the door knob, trembling with every motion.

Maybe he's watching a porno, I said trying to convince myself.

"Ah, D-a-l-e." These words came in between sounds of moaning and gurgling.

I pushed the door open and was

shocked by the scene that was taking place in Dale's bed. It was dark in the room, so I had to wait for my eyes to adjust. Dale and the woman were so wrapped up in each other they did not notice me standing in the doorway at first.

The pair was in the sixty-nine position. The woman was lying on her back and Dale was straddled above her going to town in between her straddled legs. He was so lost in sucking, licking and fingering his company that he did not pay attention to me coming closer and closer.

Dale's body began gyrating and he collapsed on top of the woman's body as he came in the woman's mouth and face.

"Baby, I thought you said you were going to let me know before you were gonna cum," the woman said, laughing.

It wasn't until her trifling ass she sat up and tried to push him off of her that I seen Eva's face.

All sounds of laughter suddenly went away as Eva opened her eyes and saw me standing damn near over the bed.

My heart dropped into the pit of my stomach.

"Dale, get up."

So many things were running through my head. Should I yell, scream, fight? What the hell do I do? I was at a lost for words.

"Baby, what's wrong? I know you are not--" Dale couldn't finish his sentence. It took his dumb ass a while but he finally noticed me standing there.

"D!"

"I'm sorry I interrupted."
I started with a new set of tears flowing down my face. "I just came to tell you that Ashley followed me to David's to tell me she's having your baby. "

You better call her.

Congratulations...Daddy.

The door was open, that's why I came in."

I paused and took in a deep breath finally getting the nerve to speak to the pair. Neither one of them attempted to move a muscle.

Before I caught a case, I turned and began to walk out the door.

"Tell your baby mama to stay the hell away from me," I spat at his goofyball ass.

I looked Eva dead in her eyes as I told her, "And, Eva, bitch, this shit ain't over."

I was so hurt. She is supposed to be my best friend. I am kinda glad that all this time has lasped since the last time I seen her.

My anger has subsided, but the pain has not went away. I don't think it ever will. I know that we go through obstacles everyday for a reason, but this one I can honestly say that I was not ready for.

I shook my head trying to focus on my sitation at hand. I am going to get my chance to speak to Eva, and tell everything that is on my heart. Until then....

I stood up as the nurse entered the room. I asked her what was Tiana's status, and what were they planning on doing to try to have her on the road to recovery.

I listened to the plan of action, and watched as the nurse checked her vital signs and gave her a breathing treatment. After she was gone, it was just the two of us and I talked to Tiana all night until I fell asleep.

I stretched and scratched my head, glancing around the room for a clock.

Nine forty-eight. Dang, David was going to kick my butt. He told me to come by the shop early before he had any customers.

"Hey, girl," I said, bending down kissing Tiana's hand. "I am still here. I have to run home, get dressed, and feed Dior. I promise that I will be back as soon as possible."

I waited for her to respond. I wanted her to move her fingers, see her eyelids twitch, or something. I hated seeing her like that. I prayed another silent prayer and gathered my things. I kissed her on the forehead one more time and headed home.

Unfinished Business

Rain

"We have a lot of unfinished business," kept running through my head. I had been calling Zay for the last couple of days before he stopped answering my calls.

I was sitting Indian style on the floor, holding my cell phone in my hand. I wanted to call him again, but his mailbox was full and not allowing me to leave any more messages.

My body craved for Zay terribly. I didn't know what happened. I played my part, doing everything that I needed to show him that I was by his side while he was hurting behind that bitch.

I hated her and I didn't even know why. She disappeared on his ass, and he was all up inside of me. But, the moment that she told him that she needed to talk to him because they had *unfinished business*, he was on the first thing smoking back to Las Vegas.

Laying back, I imagined the last time that he was inside me, sending sensations throughout the entirety of my body.

"Rain!" I could still hear him yell as I collapsed on top of him. I knew that he reached a climax that I had never given him before, and was prepared to give to him over a duration of an eternity.

I knew that it was not the right time

and that I was asking the inevitable, but at that point, I really did not care. I was risking my friendship with his sister to share moments like those with each other, and I needed to know what the ending verdict was going to be.

You see, I read the text message conversation between him and Dionni a couple of days prior, and I was on a mission. A mission of making him fall in love with me.

I had been in love with Zay ever since I was a little girl. Sasha, his baby sister that he raised, was my best friend.

When I was young, I used to pretend that we were married, and once I reached my teen years Zay didn't know it, but he was the one that took my virginity.

I held a picture of him that I stole from their house in front of me as I sat down on a dildo that I found in my mother's drawer. It hurt like hell, but after a couple of moments of getting my rhythm together, it actually felt good.

I was in love with everything about him. He reminded me of a long haired Shemar Moore from *The Young And The Restless*.

I knew that my informing him of my knowledge of Dionni would let him know that I secretly read his text messages, but at that point I did not care.

"Zay," I started, my voice sounding dry and husky. "Are you really leaving me to see Dionni?" I asked him while my head still rested upon his chest.

Zay never answered my question as I listened to the beating of his heart intensify.

His silence spoke to me. His silence gave me the clarification that I needed. Instead of responding, he pulled the blanket up and covered our bodies, wrapping his arms around my back.

I didn't know what to say. Tears sprung to my eyes as I took in a deep breath. My mind began to go into over drive thinking of a plan to keep Zay in my corner.

"May the best woman win," I said under my breath and closed my eyes. The game was only starting.

The next morning, we checked out of The Rosewood Mansion and returned back to our lives, leaving the weekend love affair nestled inside the suite we shared in that beautiful hotel.

Xavion Grey was running back to the arms of a woman that could not possibly love him as much as I did. I wanted him to marry me. Why didn't things work out the way that they did in the movies?

"You are so stupid!" I screamed out into the empty room. I had just moved back to Las Vegas, setting up shop in a low budget apartment on Twain and Swenson. I quit my job and drove the two day trek back to Las Vegas. I called Zay once I arrived and told him that I had nowhere to go.

"I am pregnant, Zay, and I wanted to be close to you," I stumbled out after he questioned my reasons of my sudden move.

"Pregnant, Rain, really?" he asked me after a pregnant pause. "Well, I hate to be like this, but in the words of Trey in *Menace To Society*, it can't be mine because I had the jimmy on extra tight." He then let out a soft chuckle. "How old do you think that I am? I am not one of those young ass knuckle heads that you mess with. If you are pregnant, sweetheart, you must have already been pregnant. I do feel sorry for you and all, and wanted to help you because your parents cut you off, but I promise you can't punk me into taking care of you. Some of the best have tried and they all have failed. Well anyway, if you don't have anything else real to say, then, I must say bye."

Zay then hung up on me and had not answered the phone for me since then.

"Well, like I said, may the best one win!" I screamed out, tears flowing down my face. "You are going to be with me, Zay! You are going to be with ME!"

How the Cookie Crumbles

Suave

"North Las Vegas police are asking for the public's help for any details in regards to home invasion that took place last Wednesday night in a suburban North Las Vegas neighborhood."

"Baby, come here, hurry up."

"Tonight on Action News, we are going to give you an update on that home invasion that has left a young woman fighting for her life at UMC tonight. North Las Vegas police are asking for the public's help in finding out what happened.

"Police say that Tiana Jones made it to her home on the 2300 block of East Rome Boulevard about 5:30 p.m. on September 1st. It is believed that the suspects were already inside the residence when the attack took place.

Anyone with information on may have happened to Tiana, you should call North Las Vegas police at 702-633-9111. There is a $10,000 reward for anyone that may have any information."

Suave went into the room midway through the news broadcast munching on an Oreo cookie. He smiled to himself while his girlfriend, Angel, stayed glued to the television.

"Baby, isn't that so sad? I guess we do need to get those pit bulls. That shit could have happened here. Poor girl."

Suave turned and went back into the kitchen.

Taste like….

Candy

"Hey, you, I am on my way to the house. How is Tiana doing? Has Twan been by there? Well, call me later and let me know. I love you, baby."

I hung up the phone and tossed it into my purse. I didn't like the fact that he was going to check on her by himself, but I didn't want any reason to run into Dionni. Not yet anyway.

I didn't know how she would feel

knowing that Dale and I were together, but I couldn't wait to see her face when she found out. I just had to make sure that my plan was complete before she did.

That bitch took the only real family that I had away from me in a blink of an eye, and I promised my dead Mama's grave, that bitch was going to endure the same amount of pain and anguish that I had to endure.

I was tired from my afternoon of shopping at the Forum Shops inside the Ceasar's Palace on the Vegas strip. It was Dale's birthday, and I wanted to go all out for him. I still could not believe how much Dale had gotten under my skin. I smiled to myself, visualizing the strength of his back. Damn, I loved his back. Faithfully, I volunteered every night to massage his creamy skin. I plotted and planned my get back at Dionni mission for a while now, and everything so far had been falling into place.

In the beginning, my plan was so simple. I was going to crush Dionni's heart, and that was it. No getting attached, emotional, falling in love, nothing. I had a game plan that was as smooth as any coach that stood on the sidelines at the Super Bowl, and I intended on getting my championship ring.

I tracked Dionni for a couple of weeks, familiarizing myself with the ins and outs of her day to day life.

I had her schedule down pact!

I would watch her come out of her perfect house, walk her perfect dog, go to her perfect job, hang out with her perfect friends, and then go home to her perfect man. That shit got sickening. No one's life was like that except hers. That angered me even more!

She destroyed my world and left

Zay's ass high and dry, but fell right back into the arms of another well to do black man. The first time I followed her to Dale's house and saw how the brother was living pissed me off even more.

There were so many women in the world wishing that they could get men on the levels of Zay and Dale, and were stuck with a loser man that barely made it out of his own Mama's house to lay his head down in hers without a pot to piss in. But, that trick got two successful men back to back! Now, what part of the game was that?

That was why it was my duty to give that bitch exactly what she deserved!

The first time that I laid eyes on Dale outside of Dionni's office, I knew that I had to have a piece of him. He was tall, dark, and handsome. I was impressed. He looked better up close with his Colgate smile. I handed him my card that night and told him to call me. I took it up a notch by showing up in his neighborhood to secure the house across the street that was for rent. The best part of it all was that it so happened to have the mailbox right in front!

Since all my furniture was in California, my move was easy. It consisted of me transferring my clothes and toiletries by car, and having Rent A Center deliver a dining room table, sofa, love seat, washer and dryer, and bedroom suite.

It took about a week for Dale to finally notice me. I made sure that I was out of sight, out of mind. I waited for him to go out and wash his car (his typical Saturday morning ritual) and headed out to the mailbox. I intentionally tried to open my assigned box with the wrong key.

"Um, excuse me," I called out, waving him over. "Can you help me?" I set the scene for the moment from hair all the way down to my feet. He jogged over, asking me what was wrong. "I am sorry to bother you, ugh, I am sorry. What's your name? I am Candice."

We exchanged small talk, and it didn't take long for him to realize that I was the same woman he met outside of Dionni's office. I asked him over for dinner, and he quickly informed me that he was in a relationship. I flashed him a look of disappointment and told him the offer would always be on the table. I felt his eyes on my ass as I walked away. I was hoping that it was going to be easy, but it was okay. I loved a challenge.

I began watching from the privacy of my own window, the comings and goings of the pair. It seemed like she was there every day, but it did not last for too long. Dionni stopped showing up.

After about two weeks of not seeing

her, I stopped him one morning as he was leaving. I asked him how everything was going and that was when he informed me that he and his fiancée had just broken up.

I was his shoulder to cry on, and the rest was history!

I started the ignition and attempted to back out, but I could not make myself put the car into reverse. I felt light-headed and faint. My heart was racing as images of everything that has taken place over the last six months ran through my head.

I went after Dale because of Dionni, but there was another reason as well. A reason more powerful than getting even with a high sidity acting bitch.

You see, I had been with Zay for a long time, well, let's put it the right way. I had been *working* for him a long time. Ever since Sasha was a little girl, I was

Zay's puppet.

I helped him raise his baby sister, babysit his flock of young prostitutes, making sure the money kept flowing, and maintained the upkeep of the house.

Yes, Zay wa a pimp, matter of fact, one of the biggest, high class pimps in Las Vegas. Let me rephrase that, he *used* to be one of the biggest pimps in Las Vegas. He met Dionni, and once he lost her to the game, he supposedly had seen light and walked away cold turkey.

Ok, I had to keep it real. I actually presented the idea of soliciting myself to Zay, but he never said no. He quickly accepted the money that I presented to him night after night after night. He had no objections whenever I would add another pretty face to the equation. He sat quietly as his pockets grew fatter, putting himself and Sasha through school.

Once she graduated from high

school and went off to college, he distanced himself from me and moved me to California. He would tell me on so many occasions that the move was a good thing. He wanted me to establish my own identity, whateva the fuck that meant.

"I knew I should have never left," I muttered under my breath, stepping on the brake. "If I would have stayed at home, none of this shit would have ever happened."

I mean, look at me. I was five feet, nine inches and was proud to say, thicker than a snicker. I had the perfect, exaggerated hour glass figure and smooth, deep chocolate skin.

Everywhere I went, I made heads turned whenever I walked by. I was a show stopper, and I wanted everyone to know it.

The crazy part was that everyone did. Everyone in the world knew that I was a commodity. Everyone except Zay.

At that point, I didn't care what he wanted. Well, that's what I kept telling myself.

I *had* what I wanted. I had a man that knew how to *appreciate* me. But, was I satisfied? Hell no! My plan would not be complete until Dionni and Zay knew that something that was as sweet as candy could make their lives shatter right before their eyes.

I Am Not My Hair

Dionni

Before I could reach the door of David's salon, he met me outside and scooped me up in his arms, hugging me close.

"Chile, I am so happy to see you! You had me so worried about you, girl! I know that you are on your own time table and have been running like a chicken with your head cut off, but damn, D! Three days later? I have been trying to catch up with you at home and at the hospital. How do you manage for me to keep on missing you?"

As we entered the salon, I was greeted by so much love. I know it had been a long time. I had been going in there once a week ever since he graduated from hair school and bought the shop, and I never missed an appointment.

It was because of David that my hair was as healthy as it was. It hung midway down my back, full of life and body. I would always get complimented on my locks. Some even bold enough to ask if it was real. I would always reply yes, and hand them David's card. I was his walking billboard. Well, I used to be. Ever since I had been in New York, I have been rocking a ponytail. My tresses were in need of David's pampering, so I eagerly sat down in the chair.

"G-u-r-l!" Shonni, one of the older stylists, started off. "Eva tried to waltz her nasty ass up in here the other day while David was out and about. I told her we don't welcome maggots around here, and I suggested that she started to go and find a new stylist down there where the rest of her tacky ass kind is at. Downtown, close off of Fremont, where the true low budget hoes hang out!"

Everyone in the shop both burst out laughing except for David. His face was full of concern as he watched my reaction. I assured him that I was good. Wrapping the cape around my neck, he began giving my hair the treatment that it has been lacking.

The shop was buzzing as everyone added their dose to the daily gossip. I sat quietly, half listening. Occasionally, I would smile or let out a soft laugh, trying to pretend that everything was okay.

The last couple of days had been stressful as hell for me. I had been at the hospital, the police station, and then back to the hospital. I wanted to be there when Tiana woke up, but at that point, I was just praying that she would just wake up.

The police didn't have any leads, and Antwan's punk ass still hadn't been at the hospital. The police were starting to get apprehensive, which was making me apprehensive on where exactly *was* Antwan.

They put out a missing person's report for Anwan, and I hade also issued a reward. I was hoping that once the reward was announced on the news, that we would get closer to solving the case, but it did just the opposite. The police were getting leads, but all turned out to be insufficient.

"So, what look were you looking for? David asked while rinsing the deep conditioner out of my hair.

"Um, I was thinking about trying something new. I saw this cute style on tv, that I know you can handle. Hold on, let me see if I can find it in one of these magazines."

I was nervous about telling David I wanted to cut my hair off completely. I knew that he was going to over react, so I had been mentally trying to prepare myself for it.

"I have thought about this look since I seen Monica on her reality show rocking it. Her facial structure is about the same as mine. Don't you think? So, I am not worried about how it was going to look on me. What do you think?"

David stood in disbelief as I spoke. "Cut your hair? Are you serious?"

"Yes, baby, I am serious. I need this, David. I don't know how to explain it. I think it will empower me. I have been having an emotional battle with myself, and I believe that if I am ever going to get over all this negativity, I am going to have to start by shedding... my hair."

We sat in silence for a few moments before David finally spoke.

"Okay, heifa... which side do you want to be the bang to be on? The left or the right?" He kissed my forehead and proceeded with cutting my hair.

Please, come back to me

Antwan

I waited until I saw Eva get into her car and leave the parking lot before I made my entrance to the hospital. It had been my daily ritual for the past two weeks.

I wait until everyone left before I went inside to check on Tiana. I had been doing that every day. Right now was not the time for anyone to see me.

I was trying to put together the missing pieces of what happened to my baby. I knew Suave had his hands all up in it.

And, he had every right to want to hurt me. I lost twenty five stacks of that dude's money. I would have put out a hit for me as well if I was him, but to hurt T?

I never thought that he would go that far. I wished I could turn back the hands of time. I want to go back to the day that I met Suave. If I knew then what I knew now, I would have went home to the arms of the one who loved me.

I had done all kinds of dirt in the past, but none of them had paid me as well as this one had. I counted cards.

Everyone wanted to mess with me, too because I was a one man show. I was considered "The Big Player." I knew how to confuse the hell out of the dealer. I would take my time and lose my money over hours and hours of mediocre playing.

I would win a couple of thousand, and then end up losing several more. In reality, I was a Spotter who had Gorilla money. I know I lost you with the terminology. Let me break it down.

A Spotter was the one that counted the cards. I was a genius when it came to numbers. Back in the day, I was the kid whose math teacher knew I had potential, just didn't apply myself in my other classes.

A Gorilla went to the casino with a lot of money and bet big all the time. That was where Suave came in. He provided the cash for me so that I would use my counting talent, bet with my large bank roll, and hit these casinos for thousands of dollars a night.

In the beginning, I used to just go down to the small casinos on Boulder Highway and win a couple of thousand of dollars a night. I should have been satisfied. I was bringing in steady money every night, and I wasn't robbing the house (the casino). But no, I got greedy. And, you know what they said about being greedy.

Well, I met Suave one night during a Blackjack tournament. We were there for over eight hours, staying in the top five rankings. I knew that I could have won, but I was getting tired. I offered a split of the winnings while I was winning, and everyone accepted their payout.

That was when Suave approached me. I felt him watching me all night, that was normal. After a tournament, I would get dirty looks from some of the gamblers, or some would try to befriend me.

Suave was different.

He congratulated me, offered me a drink, and asked me how did I learn how to play Blackjack like that. I informed him that it was easy because I just had a gift with numbers.

We both ordered a shot of Remy, and he told me to jot down his number. We threw those drinks back and headed out to the parking lot.

I ended up calling him a week later and we met up at a local P T's pub, and I guess that was when he gave me my mock interview. He asked me if I would like to go into business with him. He said that he would provide me at least five thousand dollars at a time to bet with. As long as I flipped it, I could have the five stacks. Now, remember when I said my teacher would say that I had potential? That was all I had. I didn't read between the lines.

No warning signs flashed in my head. I just agreed and went along with it.

That was a start of a beautiful relationship. With Suave supplying the money, I was able to bet at a higher scale, which in turn allowed me to win more. Suave kept adding more and more money to the package that he gave me nightly, and insisted that I started going to the strip casinos.

That was until the night before that shit happened to Tiana. That night he gave me twenty five thousand to bet with, and I lost everything. I never lost. On a bad day I may break even, but never had I lost my complete bankroll.

I felt like I was set up, but I didn't know how to prove it. Now Suave was after me. I tried to explain to Tony what happened. He was the one that dropped off and picked up the cash from me nightly. Tony didn't say a word. He informed me that Suave would get back to me, and left. I hadn't heard from either one of them.

I didn't go home. I went back to the casinos that I knew and tried to raise the money back. When I called Tiana the next morning and her phone kept going to voicemail, I had a bad feeling that something happened.

I went home, but was greeted by a police barricade on my block. I reversed out of my neighborhood and rode around. Now here we are. Two weeks later, and my baby was still lying up in that hospital not opening her eyes or moving.

I wanted to kill Suave. I wanted someone to do the same damage to him that he did to my baby. After all those months of my making so much money for that clown, and he hurt my baby?

I stood over Tiana's bed, praying for her like I did every night. "Baby, come back to me, please? Baby, wake up." Tears dripped down my face as I waited for a response. I leaned down to kiss her forehead, but froze in my position. *Did her eyes just flutter?* I waited a few more moments, whispering sweet nothings into her ear and watching her eyes. After several moments, there was the flutter again. "Come and back, baby. Come on," I continued to talk to her. I told myself I was not going to leave again until she woke up. I had to be a man and quit hiding. I needed to be there when she woke up.

The Infamous Xavier Gray

Dionni

There was a long line ahead of me as I waited in my car for a valet attendant. It was a Friday night and Town Square, an exclusive shopping center filled with exclusive shops, fine dining restaurants, and upscale lounges, was packed with locals and tourists.

"Sorry, ma'am," the young attendant said to me as he hurried and opened the door. He was out of breath and his face was flushed as I handed him the keys to my 745 BMW.

"It's okay," I replied and asked him to point me in the direction of the Cadillac Ranch.

As I strutted into the restaurant, I felt that all eyes were on me as I headed toward the lounge area. My head instantly began to nod to the sound of Kindred and the Family Soul playing in the background.

I knew I looked good in my cream D&G tank dress. Accompanying my French manicured toes were a pair of saddle brown and gold gladiator stiletto heels. My make-up was immaculate and my fragrance was by Marc Jacob.

I couldn't wait for Zay to lay eyes upon the new me. The old Dionni was chic and sophisticated as well, but this new Goddess had a slightly different twist about her. The new Dionni was no longer secretly insecure and mentally abused. There was a difference in my walk, and I held my head higher than before.

It took my eyes a few moments to adjust to the dim lighting of the room as I skimmed through the crowd trying to catch a glimpse of Zay.

Butterflies began to pitter-patter through the pits of my stomach the moment I laid eyes on him. The sexual attraction that we possessed for each other lassoed me from across the room, and instantly moistened the area in between my legs. My grip intensified on my sable clutch and I ran my tongue slightly across my lips. *Why did you let this man go again?* I thought to myself as my gorilla instincts were beginning to take over. He didn't notice me as I watched him give the waitress his order.

I stepped in closer, taking in the moment. I have had dreams about seeing Zay again. Some were beautiful while others ended up being nightmares.

Zay had sent me so many emails and text messages, trying to make sense of his crazy life. He explained to me how his parents passed and he had to take care of his sister. He went into detail, telling me the story of how he met Candy and how the prostitution began. I read every email and text message that he sent me. At first, I thought he was full of shit, but it never stopped me from reading his correspondence.

Even though I was mad, I couldn't get him out of my system. I felt like I was living Musiq Soulchild's song *Half Crazy*.

Don't get me wrong. I was devastated about Dale and Eva. That situation really did take a whole on me, but I couldn't lie, it was expected. My Grandmother always said, *When you lie with dogs, you will wake up with fleas.* When I was young, I did not understand what she meant, but now, I heard her loud and clear.

Zay's emails were so consistent. I just knew that he was going to give up. But, he didn't.

The email that made me start having second thoughts about Zay was the one addressed to Candy. I printed that one and kept it in my wallet. It was my reassurance that Zay was not that bad.

Candy,

What's up, how are you doing? Well, as for me, I guess you can say I am alright, considering the obvious. I am sorry that it has taken so long for me to contact you. No special reason that it took so longer other than trying to get my thoughts together before I just drafted a letter.

First off, I would like to say that you have disappointed me. I know that you are a grown woman, and as well, a human being, so you are allowed to make mistakes, but through all of the shit that we have been through, I truly believed that I had a genuine friend in you. This is almost impossible to come by nowadays.

The first couple of days after you left, I was lost and really couldn't believe that you were the cause of so much confusion in my life. I would like you to know that your services are no longer needed. I do not feel as if I would be able to trust you again

after that performance that you put on.
Please, do not attempt to contact me any
further. If you do not understand this
letter, then feel free to contact me via email.

It would be in your best interest if
you stayed away from me and my family.
There is no love loss, you still hold a special
place considering all of the history that we
have shared. You were there for Sasha,
and I thank you. All good things come to
an end eventually, but I didn't know our
relationship was going to end like this.

I am sorry to be so formal, but I think
in this situation, it has to be. I promise
you, Candy, that if you do not adhere to
this letter, I will have legal actions placed
against you. I will have you evicted from
your home, and everything that I allowed
you to utilize because of our business
relationship will be repossessed.

You signed that disclaimer when
Sasha graduated agreeing to these terms,

and I promise you, I will use that
documentation in court.

It was fun while it lasted.

Zay

After reading those words, I just knew I needed to see him again. I needed to hear everything that he had to say. He removed himself from that lifestyle. I couldn't lie, I was definitely opposed to prostitution, but from him to walk away from it cold turkey, I had to see for myself. I needed to look into his eyes as he explained.

Maybe it was the pent up sexual frustration that I had been having for the past six months that had me tripping, but damn! Zay was sexier than ever!

Finally, he noticed me watching him as I got closer. The smile that he shot me was so bright and genuine. I could feel the love that he still possessed for me radiating from his eyes, and damn, that felt good. I was ready to call the dinner over and take him back to my house. I needed to show him just how much I missed him.

Once I reached the table, he engulfed me in his arms. His cologne smelled so masculine but sweet, making the moisture located in between my legs go from wet to splash!

We sat down and ordered our food. He spoke and I listened, never breaking our eye contact.

He confessed his love and I confessed mine. He told me that he told himself that as long as he knew that I loved him still, he was not going to stop until he had a ring on my finger. Zay broke the steady flow of conversation, sitting back in his chair. He tilted his head to the right, absorbing every line in my face.

"Dionni, I have just one question for you, and, please, be honest as you answer," he began, running his index finger around the rim of the shot glass. "If you really started to love me, how was it so easy to let me go and run back into the arms of that clown?"

Just that quick, his facial expressions changed. Zay's face read hurt, anger, and confusion. I had never seen him like that before. Zay had never showed me emotion. He would tell me how he felt, but I constantly second guessed it because I never felt the love that he expressed he had. Well, never expressed it, until now.

The look that he gave me was one that I wanted to think about before I gave him my answer. I knew that I hurt him when I disappeared from his life completely, but let's not forget what caused me to dip out, either.

If you're going to move forward, you have to leave the past in the past, I told myself, I didn't want to talk about that. "Zay, pay for the bill and let's go. I am parked in valet. Where are you parked?"

"My truck is parked on the top floor of the parking garage. You want to go get your car and pull over there?"

"Yes, I'll meet you there." I gathered my clutch and hurried to valet.

Shenanigans

Zay

I didn't know what Dionni had up her sleeve, but I was ready to find out. She was looking so good in that dress, and I was ready to see if she had anything underneath. It felt like an eternity for the waitress to return with my card. I couldn't believe my body responded to her like that.

Dionni could still hold her own in a crowd. She possessed the same amount of sexiness and poise. And man... That hair cut. It was so beautiful. It was like she was the same person with a hint of mystery. All the love that I had for her that I thought was hidden within me released the moment I set eyes on her.

"Here you go, sir," the waitress said, interrupting my lustful thoughts. "Is there anything else that I can do for you?" she asked in a husky voice, handing me card and receipt.

I mumbled a quick thank you while signing a fifteen dollar tip on the bottom of the receipt. I flashed a half smile and hurried to the parking garage.

Once I reached my truck, Dionni was already there leaning against my passenger door. I played with my tie as I inched forward. I was so excited that she wanted to stay with me, and grace me with her presence.

"Are you going to unlock the door and let me or or not?" Dionni said softly. I unlocked the car door and watched her get in. I hurried over and closed the door behind her.

Scurrying to the driver's side, I got in and started the ignition, releasing the sound of smooth jazz from my speakers. Dionni reached up and ran her hand down my hair until she was clutching my ponytail.

My emotions confused me as my hand drifted toward hers. I was excited that she was there with me, but all the while nervous.

"Zay, can you do me a favor?" Dionni asked, her voice barely above a whisper. "Can you kiss the back of my neck like you used to do? I watched her as she turned to face the window and curve her neck forward.

Why is she doing this to me? I

thought as I watched her for a few more moments. I took a couple of deep breaths and leaned in toward her, taking in her scent.

"Damn, I missed you, baby," I said slowly and seductively. A deep moan escaped from Dionni's throat, making my animalistic senses awake.

I kissed her neck again, that time running my tongue across her shoulder blades, making my testosterone levels go into overdrive.

I looked around the parking lot to see if there was anyone around us. The window tint on my truck was limo, so I wasn't worried about anyone looking in; I just knew what I wanted to do to her and didn't need anyone to see the Escalade rocking like a boat.

In less than a second, I had Dionni nestled onto all fours as I began to massage the muscles in her legs. As I made my way down to her feet, I removed her shoes.

Dionni never missed a beat. She adjusted her weight against the window with her left hand, reclining the seat with her right. I rubbed my way back up her legs, separating them slowly. Her moaning became intense, her breathing heavy. Softly, I pushed her dress around her waist as I spread butterfly kisses around her hips and ass.

"Damn, baby, I missed you, too," Dionni crooned.

Her back began to arch as she cupped both of her breasts.

"Shhh," I replied as I removed her thin thong panties. They were soaking wet as I dropped them to the floor.

I teased her pussy slowly, inserting one finger at a time. Her mound was getting wetter and wetter by every stroke. I closed my eyes as I continued to tease

Dionni, licking her clit softly and slowly. She was losing control as her body became one with my hand, bouncing and grinding in the same motion.

I watched Dionni's expression through the car window as she enjoyed the stimulation that I was giving her. I dipped my fingers into her succulence, and then into my mouth.

Dionni's body was trembling as I began to unbuckle my pants. My dick wanted so badly to feel her, have her juices and berries run down my shaft.

Someone knocked on my passenger side window, making Dionni's body tense up. She screamed, pulling away from me.

"Oh my gosh, we got caught," I mumbled underneath my breath, straightening my clothes. We were caught alright, but not by the mall's security.

Rain's face suddenly appeared outside my window. She just stood there with her arms folded across her chest, waiting for me to respond.

This bitch is crazy, I thought, not knowing what to do. I felt like I was experiencing deja vue. That was how I lost Dionni the last time behind Candy's crazy ass acting all psychotic and shit. Now, here comes Rain doing the same shit on a different day... Boy, I sure knew how to pick those broads.

"Do you know her?" Dionni finally questioned, pulling up her panties. "Do you, Zay?"

She didn't give me a chance to respond as she grabbed her purse and hopped out of my truck. I was not about to lose her that easy. I opened my door and pushed past Rain.

"D, wait!" I yelled, jogging toward her car.

Dionni started her car while rolling down the window.

"Zay, fix that," she said, pointing in Rain's direction. "I know that I am just coming back in after several months, so I can't trip. But, if you want me to continue to be here and our relationships grow, I need you to give me your all. That is all that I am asking."

She rolled up the window and backed out. My shoulders hung as I watched her drive away. I took a couple of deep breaths and headed back to my truck. Rain was still standing there, but that time with a smile on her face.

"How long have you been out here, and how did you even know that I was here? Are you following me?" Rain rushed toward me, trying to wrap her arms my neck. "Get your hands off me and answer my questions," I demanded, getting into my truck.

"Zay, why are you acting like this?" Rain exclaimed as the tears welled up in her eyes.

"Rain," I said between clenched teeth. "Stay the hell away from me, okay?"

I then, too, rolled up my window and backed out of the parking stall, turning off my radio. I needed silence to think.

"What the hell did you get yourself into?" I screamed at the top of my lungs. I needed to fix it and quick before I lost my baby again behind that bitch and her shenanigans.

Am I Getting Punk'd?

Dionni

I was so pissed. Why did that keep happening to me with Zay? The last time it was Candy that walked in on us, now some young girl? Who was that girl?

I looked down at my speedometer to see that I was doing eighty-five miles per hour. *Slow down, girl*, I thought as I exited the freeway on Charleston and headed in the direction of the FBI building. There was a 24 Hour Fitness located inside, and how I was feeling, I could use a good workout to clear my mind.

Zay was blowing my phone up so much that I had to put it on silent. I needed to think things through without any interruptions.

I pulled up to the parking garage and pushed the button for my validation ticket. The lever went up, letting me inside the garage and I pulled into a stall.

Once I turned off my car, I laid my head down on my steering wheel, remembering my first encounter with Candy.

I didn't know what to do. Even though I was naked and covered in Zinfandel, yes the wine, I couldn't move. I was caught like a deer in headlights. That was how tonight felt.

I opened my eyes and a brown skinned girl was standing there looking at me with a peculiar look on her face. If was as if she knew who I was and was studying my face.

Both instances, I could not take my eyes off those broads. Each time waiting for the guy from *Punk'd* to jump out with the camera crew in pursuit.

At first, I thought the girl must have been a tourist or something. I knew she wasn't security or an employee of the Town Square. She just stood there, holding eye contact with me. That shit was so creepy.

Yea, I didn't know why, but the presence of the one from tonight gave me the hebegebes. There was something about her eyes. I couldn't put my finger on it, but something just wasn't right about her.

Candy had a different type of

presence about her. With Candy, the aura that she projected was one that informed you that she was going to give you a run for your money. I knew that she was the infamous Candy. That chick just stood there staring at me, but it felt as if she was looking through me.

I didn't know how to explain it. "Well, it is not for you to understand," I told myself, sitting up in my seat. I removed my heels and reached into the backseat, pulling out the pair of flip flops that I kept back there for whenever I had a long day and my feet were beginning to hurt.

Exiting my vehicle, I popped open my truck and grabbed my gym bag. It wasn't until I closed the trunk that I noticed Zay standing at the entrance.

"That's sad that I know you like this, right?" he said with a boyish grin on his face.

Even though I was pissed, a slight smile appeared on my lips. I could see why those chicken heads were acting the way they were behind him. That man was so damn fine. From the Indian grade of hair that he possessed down to the bottom of baby soft feet.

A thick cloud of awkwardness engulfed us. I didn't know what to say to him. I knew one thing though, I still had feelings for him. I needed him to get his shit together because I refused to have any more Candy type incidents between me and the women in his life.

"Baby," he started and pulled me into his arms. "I am so sorry. I am not going to lie to you though, I slept with Rain a couple of times, but that was it. I came across her when I was in Dallas, but don't you say anything crazy. She is originally from here. I knew her for a long time. But, it wasn't until Dallas that we slept together. And, yes, she does know about you, and, yes, I cut it off with her when you texted me and said that I could see you. And, no, I did not have her on the track, and, no, I do not love her. And, yes, I am in love with you."

Zay said that all in one motion. I was impressed. He held a sheepish expression as he waited for my reaction.

"So, how did she know that you were in the garage? An,d I thought you said that she was in Dallas? What is she doing all the way over here?" I asked, snuggling into his arms.

Even though I needed answers from him, I loved the way his arms felt around me. I always felt so protected.

"D," he started off, shaking his head, "that's the part that I am trying to figure out as well. I don't know what she is doing here, how she got here, and how she knew where I was at. My only answer that I can give is that she followed me. I don't know. But, I do know this, I don't want Rain, Candy, or any other big booty woman in this world. The only person that I want is you. Please, baby, let me have you."

I looked up into Zay's eyes to read his emotions. He was being so sincere.

"Okay, Zay, in the words of the Notorious BIG, I will give you one more chance, but that's it." I tilted my head up toward his, and right on cue, he placed such a tender kiss onto my lips.

He took my gym bag out of my hands and headed in the direction of my car. "I didn't know if you needed to be a member to park back here, so you are going to have to drive me to my vehicle."
I laughed out loud, shaking my head at Zay.

A sense of uneasiness still harbored my veins. *If she followed him, then she has been out there for hours,* I thought. *Only someone crazy would do that.* I unlocked my car doors and got in, but not before I scanned the parking garage looking for Rain.

I took a deep breath and got into my car.

A Room Full of Sorrys'

Eva

"I wonder if Antwan is here?" I said to myself. I was in the elevator of the hospital going to visit Tiana. It had been three weeks and she was still in there. She had come a long way, though, since her arrival, opening her eyes and mumbling little phrases.

At first, I was flabbergasted that Antwan was missing in action, but I finally caught him there a couple of days ago, talking to her and kissing her.

Where the hell have you been? was what I wanted to ask him, but it was not my place to ask any questions on what was going on. The only thing that was important to me was the fact that Tiana was awake!

The doctors and nurses informed us that she was going to be on a long road to recovery, and that it was going to a lot of bad times before it became good, but I was just happy to know that she was *on* the road to recovery.

As I got closer to the room, I heard a commotion.

Dionni, Antwan, and a nurse were in the middle of the room arguing and right in front of Tiana.

"No, this fool cannot stay here. I am listed as her next of kin, so that means I have final say on who may and may not come here to see her!" Dionni stated firmly in her matter of fact voice.

Wow! Look at her, I thought. I knew that it has been a while since I had seen D, but she had done a complete 360. She cut off her natural tresses and rocked a sultry, short cut. Her body appeared firm and shapely in a pair of black jeggings, a white tank, and red stiletto heels. Her make-up was impeccable, complimenting her fit. There was something about Dionni totally different from the last time I had seen her. Her aura projected it.

She must have felt me gawking at her from the doorway because she turned toward my direction, her eyes cold and piercing. She didn't say anything to me, however. She just went back to her conversation.

"D, I am not going anywhere," Antwan yelled, his eyes pleading with me for help. "Tiana and I are engaged, so that makes me her next of kin, not you. The only way that I am going anywhere is if Metro comes here and drags me out, but I promise you this, ma, I am staying right here."

"You know what, fool, let me call them because I think your ass has a warrant out for your arrest. I know that they would gladly come and drag you up out of here." Dionni dug into her purse, searching for her phone until she heard her name being called.

"Please, Dionni, stop," a voice, barely in a whisper said. "L-l-l-e-e-t him stay." Dionni froze in her spot, giving Tiana her undivided attention. She was trying to sit up in the bed, but kept falling backwards.

"Ma'am, can you help me with her," I said, speaking to the nurse.

It was not the time. Tiana needed all of us to get her through this. I pushed past them and hurried over to her side.

Silently, Dionni moved closer as well, and helped get put Tiana in a sitting position. The nurse hurried out to find a doctor, leaving Antwan alone in the center of the room.

"Baby, I am right here," Antwan said from his spot, not knowing what to do next. "I promise, I am not going anywhere.

Dale appeared in the doorway. "Twan, I thought you were here alone. I-I can leave and come back another time," Dale stammered, shoving his hands deep into his pockets.

"Naw, man, stay," Antwan told him. "You came to check on T because you love her just as much as everyone else in this room. You don't have to go nowhere."

Dang, it was an awkward moment. It was the first time that I had seen him since that night Dionni caught us together, and by the look on her face, it was the first time that she has seen him as well.

It was strange seeing Dionni like that. She was always so confident and collective; so seeing her in that vulnerable state was new to me. She appeared to be as innocent as a child as she struggled to not release the tears that I could tell were threatening to overflow.

All the emotions that hung in the air engulfed all of us, over powering our outer surface. I felt the tears running down my face as well as I leaned across the bed and grabbed Dionni's hand.

"Baby girl, I am so sorry," I started, not knowing what else to say. "I know I fucked up, D, I know, but I am so serious when I say that I am sorry. I miss you so much. Please, girl, accept my apology."

I was not lying to her, I really did miss her. We had been so close for so long that her absence in my life was taking a toll on me. I wished I could turn back the hands of time and start everything all over. I would not have introduced her to Dale. Hell, I would have never messed with him, either. I would just enjoy my life with Dionni, Tiana, and David. I missed that shit.

I looked at her, watching her body actions. She did not speak a word, but she did not pull away. Tiana slowly inched her hand toward ours, and I softly added hers to the equation.

We lived by the saying, "All for one, one for all, and three for five." I needed that back. I was not going to stop saying I was sorry. The two of them were my sisters, and right now we all needed each other.

What the….

Dale

When I pulled up to my house, my emotions were everywhere. I didn't know how to feel. I knew that I had hurt Dionni in the past, but in all the years that I had known her, through good or bad times, I had never seen her look at me the way she did today. I didn't even think she looked at me. It felt as if she was looking through me.

I remember when I met D, she became my best friend instantly. She became a part of my day to day routine, a part of very existence.

I could remember back when we were genuinely happy. I remember those long bubble baths and honest conversations. I tried to block Dionni out of my head, but it was so hard. I knew I pushed her away. The way Dionni looked at me let me know that there was not a possibility that we could ever get back to the way things were. I knew she didn't leave me willingly. I could honestly say that she fought for me, for our relationship. I just didn't know how to appreciate it.

So, I was given another chance at love after doing the ultimate and I still didn't know how to accept the gold that was constantly placed onto my lap.

The last couple of months, I had enjoyed Candy. She was a real woman. She knew how to take care of a man. She fed me food and pussy any time that I wanted it. She listened to me. She catered to me. She loved me.

But, do I love her back?

That was the question of the day. I knew I didn't. My mouth told her that I loved her, but my actions displayed the exact opposite.

I mean, let me be the first to admit that I knew for a fact that I did not know how to love. If I did, Raven would not be there. If I knew how to love, I would not have gotten caught up in Cali with Nia when I was supposed to be helping Candy move the rest of her belongings to Vegas. I was a poster child of a typical dog, a typical nigga. The word meant ignorant, and it took me today to realize that my very existence was that very word.

I opened the door to the garage and Candy was there to greet me, arms spread wide open. She was dressed only in a wife beater and her feet bare. Her skin smelled fresh and her face was clear. I had a dime piece and did not appreciate it.

Her smile quickly turned into a frown as she asked me where was the butter that she asked me to stop and pick up on my way home. After being in the same room as Dionni, my mind was racing. She threw off my entire equilibrium.

"Boo, I forgot. I'm sorry. I'm not hungry though. I just want to go and lay down. You want to join me?" I asked, changing the subject.

Candy sensed that I was stressed and poured me a class of Remy Martin. She was chatting to me about her day, but I sure the hell was not listening.

Quickly, I finished my drink, trying to figure out my next move. Should I just leave Candy alone and take some time to myself to reflect? I needed to figure out what I was going to do, and I knew for a fact that I was not going to be able to figure out anything up under Candy, or any woman in that manner.

"Baby, you don't look good," Candy said, finishing her own drink. "What's wrong? Let me get you into the bed." I watched her display so much compassion for me as she removed the glass from my hand, placing it on the counter. Slowly she undressed me right there, starting from the bottom of my feet.

"Mmmmm," I moaned as watched her every move. I knew I just said that I had to end our relationship, but I felt I needed to penetrate her one more time. If this shit was truly going to be over, I needed to make sure that the last time went out with a bang.

Once Candy was finished removing all of the materials from my body, I scooped her into my arms and carried her into my bedroom.

Her body trembled as I softly laid her on the pillow, staring into her brown eyes.

"What are you thinking?" Candy asked as she ran her fingers across my broad chest. She smiled at me and leaned to kiss me. "Baby, you are the one tired. I need to be making love to you." Candy tried to get up, but I wouldn't let her. I bent into her, making love to her mouth with my tongue.

The sudden gesture sent a wave of goose bumps throughout my body, catching me by surprise.

I pushed the material of the tank upward, cupping her breasts in hands. I massaged them and teased them, tenderly kissing and nibbling on each of her nipples. Candy spread her legs as far apart as possible, allowing me to play with her pussy with the tip of my dick.

"You want Daddy to put this all up into you, huh?"

Candy bit down on her bottom lip as she gave me her undivided attention. She loved when I talked dirty to her.   She sucked in a deep breath as she tried to guide my head down in between her legs.

"You want me to taste you, boo? You want me to eat this pussy?"

Candy grabbed her breasts as she nodded a shy yes. I ran my fingertips down her sides. I played with her belly button, tracing kisses inside and around it with my tongue.

By the look on Candy's face, I could see that she enjoyed the foreplay that I was putting on her. Spreading the lips of her pussy with my thumbs and fore fingers, I licked the fullness of her mound with my tongue.

Candy took in another deep breath as she grabbed my head, holding on for dear life. I had her body open to whatever I was going to put on her.

I took my time while my face was in between her legs. Candy couldn't take it anymore. Sweat was dripping from both of our bodies, and I hadn't even penetrated her yet.

Candy was so wet. I couldn't take it anymore. I reached on the side of the bed and grabbed a condom. Quickly, I applied the latex material over my dick and dug deep inside Candy. She had no control. I pushed her legs up over my shoulders, cupping the crevases of her ass as I pounded my dick deep inside of her.

Candy screamed out in pleasure as my rhythm continued. We had shared some intense moments, but I knew for a fact that I had never fucked her that way before.

"Zay, baby, wait."

The moment I heard the words

escape her lips, I was done. *Did this bitch just call me Zay? Aint this some shit?* I pulled my dick out of her and headed for the bathroom to flush my wasted condom.

When I returned, Candy was lying in the same position that that I left her in. She was lying there, staring at the wall.

"I am so sorry, Dale," she said. "I guess he is still in my system, huh?" Before I could ask her who and what the hell was she talking about, Candy spoke again. "I'm sorry, Dale, and I know what you are thinking. Zay is same person that Dionni was in a relationship with."

I stood there speechless, just staring at her. *How the hell did she just call me another man, but didn't possess a bit of remorse for it? Secondly, did she just tell me that the dude is the same one that Dionni was messing with? Yes, she knew Dionni was my ex, but that was it. I never went into great detail about her.*

"If you have something to tell me, Candy, then I suggest you start explaining," I told her. "But, before you do, you got put some clothes on and meet me in the dungeon."

I did an about face and exited the bedroom, leaving Candy alone to figure out what she was going to do.

You think this is a game, huh

Suave

I listened as the phone rang and went to voicemail, and I didn't leave messages. It had been almost a month and I had been waiting patiently for the rest of my money.

When the plan was first brought to my attention, I thought it was a slam dunk. One hundred thousand dollars to do damage to a broad?

Hell yea, I was with it. But, now all this time has passed, and the news stated that the girl had come out of the coma that she was in, and all that I had was fifty stacks? Nah, I didn't do business like that.

I thought I had gotten myself in the middle of someone's personal vendetta, and I was not someone to be played with. Now that I sat back and looked at everything, the entire situation seemed like a game.

I dialed the number one more time and waited impatiently as the voicemail came on. I hung up and dropped the phone in my lap.

I needed some time to think about how I was going to clean up the mess that I had gotten myself twisted into. There was a reward out for anyone who had any leads of what happened. The girl had came out of the coma and was back at home under high surveillance of the police, and I knew that Antwan had to know that I had something to do with it.

I knew the fool was not crazy enough to go to the police, especially after all the casinos that he had hit, but that didn't mean he didn't have some plan of getting back at me.

Yea, I needed to think about my next move before I made it.

My phone rang, interrupting my thoughts. It was my girl. "Hey, baby," I answered, shaking off my thoughts.

I had to get a handle on the situation and quick. I already lost my daily hustle, losing out on Antwan. I needed to clean this up before my whole operation and livelihood went down right before my eyes.

Damn!

Candy

I got up and pulled a gown over my head. The sound of Lil John was blasting from the game room. *Damn! What am I going to tell him?* I really didn't know, but I had to tell him something and quick. I began to pace the floor, trying to think. It was some bullshit and I knew it.

Dale was ballistic, and he had every right to be.

How did I just have the audacity to call him Zay?

That was dumbest thing that I had

done in a long time. Trying to get my thoughts together, I needed to get my butt down those stairs and quick.

My cell phone started to ring, but it was not the time to answer it. Slowly, I opened the door and headed toward the game room.

Descending down the stairs, I watched Dale sitting on the sofa with his head buried into the palms of his hands. It felt like my plan was backfiring right before my eyes. I really did love Dale. I didn't want to lose him.

I didn't know why I couldn't let the beef go with Dionni. To the outside looking in, I was already the winner. She already lost Zay and now Dale, but yet, I wasn't satisfied.

I didn't know exactly what I was going to say to him, but I had to make sure that it was good. I needed to make him see that it was more than a game.

It was not supposed to be happening like that. I just knew that I had a foolproof plan. How did that BITCH manage to constantly win?

"Candice, are you just going to stand there and gawk at me or are you going to tell me what's going on? I need you to fill me in." Dale spoke slowly but steady, his fingers rubbing his temples.

I went over to the couch and sat down next to him. At that moment, I knew what I was going to tell him. I was going to tell him the truth. That was going to be the only way I was going to be able to save the fucked up situation. I hoped.

I took a deep breath and started from the beginning. I explained to him how I met Zay, and ended up living with him and his sister. How I helped raise her and slowly started working for him at the same time. Dale's body tensed up as I explained my life of prostitution, but I had to come clean. It was the only way we were going to have any kind of closure.

I continued my story, telling him how I ended up in Los Angeles. How I got enough nerve to inform Zay of my true feelings and how he humiliated me by having a threesome with another woman. I described to him my feelings of reject and humility after we were finished, and after all of that he never even touched me.

He enjoyed the show that we were giving me, but once Sophia made him cum, he dismissed me from the bedroom, and a short time later from his home as well.

I poured my heart out to Dale, sobbing as I spoke. During my time in L. A., that was when he met Dionni and got entangled in a serious relationship with her. I described to him my new plot of getting rid of Dionni. I was hurt that Zay told me to stay away from Vegas for a while so that he was able to take their relationship to the next level. That shit broke my heart, but like the puppet that I was, I did just that.

That was when I decided to take my plan to the next level. Deep down, I knew even if I got Dionni to leave that he would never be with me. But, I became obsessed.

I stopped and looked at Dale, watching his reaction. He just sat lifeless on the couch in silence. *I told him this much, I might as well tell him the rest,* I thought.

I started my story again, giving him details of how I secretly flew to Las Vegas, hired a locksmith, and broke into Zay's house. Till that day, I didn't know exactly what I was looking for, I just knew that I was just looking.

My plan was almost complete and I arranged for my own rape to get me back into the house. I knew that it was sick, but I had to do what I had to do to get my man back.

That was when my plan blew up in my face. Zay found a picture that I secretly stole from him and started to question me. That, in turn, became a heated argument that Dionni had the pleasure of walking into the middle of. She turned her back on Zay, never looking back and found herself back into his open arms.

Dale let out a deep breath and shook his head. He opened his mouth to speak, but I stopped him, placing my finger to his lips. He winched at the gesture, but I had to finish my confessions.

I concluded my story by telling him that I was the reason Tiana was in the hospital.

"The ring leader of the crew that

Antwan runs with was one of my biggest clients. I set up that loss he took and sent the goon squad after Tiana to scare her.

"I didn't know that they were going to do damage to her like that. I swear, I didn't. I just wanted to make Dionni feel the pain that I have been feeling. I am sorry, Dale. Baby, you have to believe me when I tell you that. I want to be with you, baby, I want..."

Smack!

Dale back handed me in the mouth. "Bitch, are you serious! You tangled my entire family in your plan in hopes of getting some pimp back? Get the fuck out of my house, Candy, now, and don't touch shit. Just get your keys and you get out now before I beat the hell out of you! GET OUT!"

There was so much rage in Dale's eyes, hate in his voice. I wiped the blood away from my mouth and stood up, but not fast enough. Dale forcefully pushed me toward the door.

"Baby, I'm sorry," I cried, trying to gain my balance. Why did shit like that continue to happen to me? I was trying to make things right. "Baby," I said softly as I inched toward the stairs.

Dale pointed as he assisted my exit, pushing me up the stairs. "Bitch, shut the fuck up and get the hell out of my house!"

I hurried up the stairs, grabbed my keys and my purse, and left.

Blank Stare

Sasha

It had been years since I had seen Rain. I was so excited. I called Zay, telling him that I was going to see her, but he didn't respond. He changed the subject, informing me that he would be at Dionni's if I needed him. Her friend was going to be getting out of the hospital soon, and they were setting up the downstairs bedroom for her.

We exchanged good-byes and hung

up. I sent Rain a text message, asking her to send me her address. She invited me over for dinner. She wanted to catch up and have girl talk just like we used to back in the day.

I was so excited. Rain was my childhood best friend. We went through everything together, and I mean everything. When we were growing up, kids at school used to tease her because she was different.

She was blessed to be a chocolate sistah with piercing green eyes. Her hair was long and thick, constantly parted down the middle in two braided ponytails. She came from a two parent household and both of her parents worked, but her father had a drinking and gambling problem.

He used to blow his check in the casinos and would come home and beat Rain's mom senseless. Rain made me promise that I would never tell anyone what was going on in her house. Being the good friend that I was to her, I stood true to my word. I never told anyone anything. I used to invite Rain over to keep her out of the house. I wanted her to be normal. I hated that people were mean to her.

That situation went on for years until Rain escaped to college. She got accepted to Texas Southern University on a full ride scholarship, and I had not seen her since.

I was so proud of her. She had been holding herself down for a while now. Everyone couldn't do that.

Ding. My text message notification went off. It was Rain sending me her address.

"Oh, she's close to the Boulevard Mall," I said aloud, recognizing the cross streets.

Quickly, I gathered my hair into a

lazy ponytail, grabbed my keys and purse, hurried into the garage, and hopped into my Nissan Z.

Twenty minutes later, I was exiting the 15 freeway onto Spring Mountain. I had the windows down, enjoying the warm breeze.

Ding. Another text message came through from Rain.

Girl, can you stop and get some packing tape for me. I don't have enough space for all of my things and I think I am going to have to put them in storage.

I shot her back a quick yes message and turned right on Maryland Parkway, heading to Target. *I think I am going to ask Rain to come and stay with me,* I thought. It didn't make sense for her to be living over there by herself, and I had so much room in the four bedroom townhouse Zay bought for me. "It's not going to hurt to ask," I said aloud, pulling up in front of Target.

Fifteen minutes later, I was leaving Target with packing tape, a Mahogney friendship card, and two Lipton ice teas.

I texted Rain and told her I had the tape and was on my way. When I pulled up to her apartment, I was in shock. I knew the neighborhood was older, but those apartments were horrible.

It looked like the only people that inhabited them were crystal users, pimps, and prostitutes. Getting out of the car, I forwarded Zay her address. It was an unspoken rule for me to do that.

My brother wasn't that much older than me, but he acted like an old man. "Someone should always know where you are at in case of an emergency," he would say matter of factly.

I didn't feel comfortable leaving my car outside in that neighborhood, but what was I going to do, bring it upstairs with me?

Clutching my purse close to my side, I quickly scanned the units, looking for building 25. Once I made eye contact with the building, I made a mad dash in its direction and hurried up the stairs.

I only knocked once before Rain flung the door open, screaming at the top of her lungs.

"Sasha, oh my gosh! Look at you. It is so good to see you!" Rain scooped me into her arms, pulling me close. "Girl, you look good! I see you have finally developed, having the nerves to have some hips and shit. Oh wait! Do you got a booty, too? G-U-R-L. Living down South was the best thing that happened to you, huh?"

I let out an embarrassed laugh as she spun me around giving me a once over.

"I have to admit, living in the ATL did thicken me up some, but I think it wasn't until I went to Italy with my Sorors' after graduation is what allowed my booty to get bigger."

"Italy? Gurl, shut your mouth," Rain exclaimed, leading me over to the couch. "Wow, my friend is a world renowned traveler huh? Must be nice..." Rain said in a mock singing voice.

It wasn't until I sat down that I paid attention to Rain and her living situation. Even though Rain looked the same, still possessing that to die for hourglass figure, chocolate brown skin, and beautiful green eyes, there was something totally different about her. I couldn't put my finger on it, but her entire aura was different.

Other than the couch, the room was bare. There was nothing that said home about that place. *I wonder what she need the tape for? She has more than enough*

room for whateva she's about to put into
storage.

"So... How's Zay?" Rain said, interrupting my thoughts. I looked up at her, shooting her a quick smile.

"He's fine," I quickly replied. "I spoke to him right before I got here. I told him that you were in town and I was coming over for dinner. By the way, I'm starving," I told her, looking around the kitchen. It wasn't until then that I noticed that there wasn't any hearty aromas coming from within the kitchen. "I thought you said you were cooking? Don't you hear my stomach rumbling?" I joked, rubbing my abdomen. "I have been starving myself all day just so that I would enjoy our meal tonight. Girl, why didn't you tell me there was a change of plans? I stopped and got that tape, I could have stopped across the street at Jason's Deli and grabbed us a platter of sandwiches and soup. I wonder what time they close?" I questioned, opening the Internet on my phone. All the excitement that I had earlier was quickly going away. Rain was starting to act weird. She just sat there, staring at me intensely.

"What did he say?" Rain asked, entirely ignoring my complaints of hunger.

"What did who say? The phone is still ringing." It was a blank stare moment. I was starting to think it was time for me to leave. I didn't like the vibe that Rain was giving off.

"I'm talking about Zay, girl. Fuck whoever you are talking to on the phone. What did Zay say when you told him you were coming over here?" she asked, taking me completely by surprise.

I hung up the phone and turned my attention back to her. "Um, he didn't say anything. Him and his girlfriend were going to set up her house for her friend that is getting out of the hospital. Can I ask you a question? What is up with you? Is something on your mind? Why are you cursing at me, and why all the questions about my brother?" Yes, it was time to go. I stood up and waited for her to answer my questions. "Rain, for real. What's going on?"

Before I could say another word, Rain rushed me and we crash landed into the wall. Before I could respond, the entire room went black.

Cursed

Candy

I got into my car, not knowing where I was going. Tears were streaming down my face as I started the ignition.

I told that man that I have been pimped out, raped, and beaten, and the only thing that he seemed to hear was that I went after him because of Dionni. Forget the fact that I was being a bigger woman by admitting the false pretense that I started to love him. Don't give me credit that I that I am trying to make the situation right.

"Bitch, get the fuck out of my house!" Was all that he had to say to me? I was so tired of every man in my presence that felt that they had the right to talk to me and treat me like that.

The two men in the world that I thought would never come at me in such a negative way, *both* called me a bitch behind the same woman, Dionni. I hated her ass so much. I couldn't seem to get rid of her.

I was so lost in my own thoughts that I did not realize that I was driving to Zay's house. The same house that I used to consider my home. Once outside, I parked my car across the street and stared out the window.

The circular driveway used to host all kinds of vehicles. I smiled to myself, remembering scenes from Sasha's childhood and teenage stages. She was such a good kid, never getting into any trouble. She was scared that if she did she would disappoint me or Zay.

BZZZZZZ. I damn near jumped out of my skin. When I ignored any missed calls, my phone automatically buzzed to remind me to check it.

Hoping it was Dale, I picked it up and checked the number. My hopes were let down again when I realized the missed call was from Suave.

"Oh my gosh! I forgot. Shit!" I exclaimed. I promised Suave that he would have his money by now. If it was a perfect world, Dale and I would be on good terms and I was going to get the money from him.

"Shit! Shit! Shit! Okay, think, Candy, think," I told myself, taking in a couple of deep breaths. The only other person that I knew kept the amount of money that I needed was on the inside of the very house I was sitting there staring at.

You helped that fool raise his sister and put hundreds of thousands of dollars inside of his bank account. He better help you, I thought.

Even though my mind was talking big stuff, my heart was telling me a different version of the story. My heart was pleading for me to sit my butt right where I was at or go home.

Zay's black Escalade pulled up in front of the house, making me forget about my dilemma of contacting him. I watched as Zay opened his door and hopped out of the truck, straightening the jeans that he had on.

It wasn't until he walked over to the passenger side and opened the door that I realized Zay was not alone. Tenderly, he helped Dionni get out of the truck.

Dionni! What the hell is she doing here?

The fear that I harbored of coming into contact with Zay all went away when I saw the two of them together.

Am I cursed? Am I not capable of being loved?

Why couldn't I get that man out of my mind, my heart, my soul? He was my first love. My first real friend. I needed Zay in my life and he didn't even know it.

He let me go out of his life so easily. Knowing deep down in my heart that he did not think about me was torture, and now seeing the two of them together was the slap across the face that sealed the deal.

Before I knew it, I didn't know what came over me, and I got out of my car and ran over to the couple.

"Zay! Zay!" I yelled, charging toward them like a mad woman. "What the hell is going on, Zay? I thought you were done with her like you were done with me?"

I caught them both by surprise, but I didn't care.

Zay grabbed my arm, dragging me back toward the street. "Do you think I am some kind of punk ass dude that you can just play with? You better get to explaining what the hell you are doing here, or...or, you... better yet, don't talk, Candice. Just get your trifling ass off of my property before I call the police!"

Zay was so upset, he was turning red. His chest was heaving and his eyes were starting to fill with hate.

"Call the police, and on me?" I spat into his face. I wonder if Nevada has a statue of limitation on pimping and pandering cases? How would that look that the bottom bitch testifies her long term pimp? Hmmm?"

I knew I was getting under Zay's skin. If he wouldn't let me love him, I may as well piss him off.

"Why the hell are you haunting me like this, Candy? I have done everything for you. Why can't you just oblige with my one wish and just leave me the hell alone, Candy? Why?"

While all the commotion was going on, Dionni snuck past us and got into her car. Neither of us noticed what she was doing until we heard her engine roar. She backed her car out of the circular driveway that used to be mine, and rolled down her passenger window.

"Baby, I don't have time for this. When you are done putting out the trash, come over my house. We have armed, patrolling security that handles situations like this one." Dionni rolled up her windows, speeding off.

That bitch thinks I am a joke, doesn't she? I got to show her that I am not to be played with.

I shook free from Zay's grip and jogged back to my car. I could hear Zay screaming obscenities to me, but I had my tunnel vision going. I had one thing on my mind as I started my car and skidded out behind Dionni.

Trick Please

Rain

"Good morning," I said as I opened the door to my guest bedroom. I felt terrible seeing Sasha tied up like that, but damn, I had to do what I had to do.

She was lying on her side, staring at the wall. Part. of me wanted to take a razor to the tape that I had wrapped around her upper torso, but I had to think with my head, not my heart.

"Today is the da, that we will not just be friends anymore. Hopefully by tonight, Zay will come to his senses and I will be his wife. Well, if he knew what was good for you, he will put a nice rock on my finger."

I spoke with confidence. I wanted Sasha to support me, but at that point I didn't give a fuck if she did or didn't. I had one main objective, and that was making Zay mine and no one else's.

Sasha just looked at me, eyes filled with disbelief. I had her mouth taped as well to ensure that she wouldn't bring any unwanted attention.

"Now, you do have a choice. You can stay here tied up like a crazed animal, or you can help me execute my plan. Which one do you prefer?"

I paused, giving her a moment to display some sort of a response. I paneled her face, watching for some sort of emotion, but there wasn't any.

Sasha's eyes held a blank expression, but the rest of her face held another.

"What? Do you have something to say?" I asked her, trying to read her expression. I stepped closer to her. I kneeled down and pulled the tape off that held her mouth shut. She winced in pain, but it didn't change her expression. "I am giving you a chance to speak your mind. Were you trying to tell me something? Are you having second thoughts? Are you going to help me marry your brother?"

The corners of Sasha's mouth twitched as a smile appeared on her face.

"Trick, please," she said, shaking her head. "I don't know what makes you think that my brother would want to marry your lunatic ass. He is working on his relationship with Dionni, and I can reassure you that you are no competition to her." She closed off her speech by spitting in my face.

I grabbed her by the neck, pinning her head down to the ground. *Trick, please?* I could not believe that she still had the nerve to talk shit and spit on me to me after all of this. "Sasha, I got a question. Why are you fucking with me? Do you not see what I am capable of? You think I am crazy, don't you?" I continued to apply pressure to her throat. I watched her face change from light brown to crimson. "No, bitch. I am not crazy. I am just determined. I dreamt about being with Zay for a long time." Sasha reached up to grab my hands and tried to pull it away from her neck, but she was unsuccessful. "I just got one question for you," I asked.

"Why are you taking me for a joke? How can you say that I am not competition to Dionni? You have it twisted. She is not any competition for me. T-R-I-C-K, PLEASE!"

I let go of her throat and stood up. "Please, start taking me seriously, Sasha. That is all that I ask of you." I closed the door and went to the bathroom. I stood in front of the mirror. "You can't kill Sasha, she's your sister in law," I told myself, glaring at my reflection. "Her ass better get it together then, and help me tear her brother away from Dionni," I responded to myself.

"We are on a mission and she plays a valuable role in this mission. I need her be on my side. I can't have her messing this up for me."

"SASHA, YOU ARE NOT GOING TO MESS THIS SHIT UP FOR ME, YOU HEAR

ME!" I screamed out. "YOU ARE PART OF THIS MISSION! YOU HOLD A VALUABLE ROLE. YOU ARE NOT GOING TO FUCK UP MY PLANS, SASHA GRAY!"

I slammed open the bathroom door and went back to the room that I was holding Sasha hostage in. She was lying there, not knowing what to do. Tears were streaming down her face as she watched me.

"SASHA GRAY, DO YOU HEAR ME?" I barked at her. "YOU ARE GOING TO HELP ME, RIGHT? RIGHT, SASHA, RIGHT?"

Sasha nodded in defeat, closing her eyes.   A smile crept across my lips as I watched her agree to assist me.

"Thank you, friend, thank you," I said, grinning from ear to ear. "Get some rest. We will go over our mission in the morning."

I closed the door and went into my room. I lay down across my bed and closed my eyes. In the morning, we were going to start the 'Getting my Man Back' mission. I couldn't wait.

Handling Business

Dale

"Hey, Twan. What's up with you? How's Tiana doing?" I listened to him describe her steady progress and how they were going to release her in the next couple of days with a full time nurse.

"That's cool, man, for real. Can you come outside real quick? I want to give you something, man. I am sitting out here right by the emergency entrance. Come on real quick before she wakes up, okay?"

I had been sitting out in front of the hospital for the past hour. After Candy dropped that atomic bomb on me earlier, I really needed to think. Even though Candy crossed the line, I couldn't totally blame her. In the past, I used to listen to my uncles and cousins describe stories of a woman scorned, but I never had to live it.

I couldn't lie though. Candy was extreme with the damage that she caused. I felt dumb as hell that I allowed myself to get wrapped up in her demonic plot.

She left me with a lot to think about. She made me put a lot of shit into perspective. Zay left her with a heart that was bitter and cold. She was too far gone too allow anyone one to love her.

Even though she blamed Dionni for her situation, the real culprit was Zay. That made me think about me and all the pain that I have given the different women in my life. Especially Dionni.

I used their kindness for weakness, and made them do everything and anything that I want. Even if it meant that they were belittling themselves like I did to Ashley. Break up friendships like I did to Eva. Or, just break their heart like I did to Dionni. Either way, the shit wasn't right.

Candy, Candy, Candy. If I would have just stayed away from her, none of this would have happened. She was the reason my sister in law was in the hospital.

The worst part of it was that Twan came to me like a man and asked me to help him fix it, and I didn't listen. I was more worried about him waking up Candy and I really wasn't listening. He asked me could he borrow the money so that he could call it even with his Suave. At the time, I thought the story sounded bogus.

He expressed to me that he thought he was set up and I blew the whole idea out the water. I gave him a lecture on being careless and told him that I was not going to help him out of that one.

I remembered shaking my head in pity at me brother as I climbed the stairs, leaving him alone to wallow in his thoughts. I had to help him fix it, I just hoped it wasn't too late.

I watched Antwan come out the exit doors and hurried over to my car.

"What's going on, man? Why you just didn't come upstairs? Tiana took three steps today, brother. My baby is getting stronger and stronger every day. Park the car, man, and come check her out!"

Antwan was elated. It was the happiest that I had seen him in a long time. The positive energy that he was projecting convinced me more that I was making the right decision.

"T, go back upstairs, man," I started, smiling at my brother. "I just wanted to tell you that I love you and I am proud of you. Here, man. Take care of what you need to," I told him, handing him a manila envelope."

Antwant looked down at the envelope confused.

"What's going on, Dale? What is this for?" Twan tried to read my face in search of the answers that he needed.

"Just say I squared away your financial obligation. I just left Suave, and I think we have came up a solution to ya'll's situation. I paid him what you owed and more. That's twenty thousand, man. It is more than enough to take care of that dream wedding that your girl has been dreaming for. Take care of your business, man, and quit looking over your shoulders. You are straight now, baby brother. Just promise me from this point on, you are done with the hustling. I love you, man, okay? Now, put that money in your pants and get back up there to your family."

Antwan reached over and hugged me. Tears were in his eyes when we finally released. "Thank you, Dale..." he started, but I stopped him mid sentence.

"The only way that you can repay me is allowing me to be the best man in your wedding. Now, get out my car before these folks start thinking you're my man or something."

We exchanged good-byes and Antwan got out, but not before he stuffed the money down his boxer shorts, hiding the package with his oversized white tee.

Once he was inside the building, I pulled away.

Hit and Run

Dionni

I was almost home and decided to stop on Craig and MLK at the Krispy Krème donuts. I just had got off the phone with Zay, and he was complaining that he was starving. I knew that the donuts were not food, but it could hold him over until I was done cooking.

I stood in line as I studied the menu. Even though the only thing that I ever ordered from there was a dozen glazed donuts,   I always did the same thing.

It didn't take the young girl behind the register long to get my order together. I gave her a five dollar tip as my phone rang.   I looked down at the number, debating if I should answer. Taking in a deep breath, I answered the call on the last ring.

"Yes, Dale, how can I help you sir?" I asked while gathering some napkins.

"Hey, D, I am not trying to keep you long.   First, I wanted to thank you for taking the leadership and being the bigger person allowing us to see Tiana. I know this situation has been hard on you, but you have held it down, so again, I wanted to say thank you." Dale cleared his throat, continuing his speech. "Next, I wanted to tell you I'm sorry.   I am sorry for hurting you, cheating on you, and sleeping with Eva. I am nothing without you, Dionni."

Wow, where the hell is this coming from? I thought as I unlocked my car.

"Lastly, I wanted to tell you th..." Our conversation was interrupted by the sound of tires screeching.

Turning around, I screamed, dropping my cell phone. Candy was using her car as a weapon, charging toward me at full speed.

BOOM!

"Damn, my head is spinning," I said, placing my left hand on my head. *What the...?* I thought to myself, trying to sit up. I needed to get up and get an asprin, but it felt as if a dead weight was pinning me down.

At first, I didn't recognize where I was, and started to panic. It took a moment for my eyes to adjust to the darkness and figure out I was in Zay's bed.

"Baby, what happened?" I asked Zay. "Am I tripping? I had a dream that Candy tried to hit me with her car." The last thing that I remembered was watching her speed toward me. Did Candy try to kill me? Visions of the car accident was vivid in my mind.

"Shhh baby, go back to sleep," I heard Zay whisper in my ear.

"What are you doing here, where am I? What, what happened? Baby, please, fill me in. What happened to me? Where's Candy?"

A thousand questions were running through my head as I tried to remember what happened. I knew that I was on the phone listening to Dale apologize when I heard the car coming toward me.

I lowered my eyes as tears began to set in the corners. That woman tried to kill me because she wanted him that badly. Was the relationship worth it?

Zay must have been able to read my thoughts. He pulled me closer to him, holding my body tight.

Mmmmm. I love how his arms feel around me.

"Baby, Candy is in jail," he informed me. "She tried to hit you with her a car, but one of the patrons leaving Krispy Krème, witnessed what was happening and pulled you out of harms away. And, thank God. I don't know what I would have done if I lost you."

I wanted Zay to protect me. I wanted him to take away all the hurt and pain that Candy had set in my heart.

I opened my eyes, gazing into Zay's. "So, she did hit my car? Is she okay? Did you get the information of guy that saved me? I want to thank him." I stated to him, my voice barely a whisper.

"Yes, baby, I got his info," Zay replied, smiling. He kissed both of my eyelids, and ran soft, sensual, reassuring kisses down my face, neck, and chest. "All I know is that Candy is still breathing. The exact status of her state currently is not important to me right now. By the time I got there, they had already rushed her to the hospital. I mean, how well can she be doing? She hit a car head on. She is not going to have an easy road to recovery."

I released a deep sigh, wrapping my arms around his neck. I separated my legs apart in a V position, inviting him to come in.

He accepted my offer, removing my panties from my body. Softly, he rubbed my body parts. He licked two of his fingers and caressed my clit. He repeated the motion over and over again, never taking his eyes off of me, ensuring my enjoyment.

"Baby, you are safe now," Zay whispered between kisses. "Thank you for not leaving me again behind that crazy bitch. I promise you from this moment on, I am going to do everything in my power to show you just how much I appreciate you."

Slowly, Zay pulled me up into a seated position. He got off the bed and knelt down on the floor beside it.

"Baby, will you marry me?" Zay asked, holding both of my hands. "I cannot afford to lose you again. Please, baby, marry me."

I didn't know what to say. He caught me by surprise. Suddenly, a smile spread across my face as I leaned in. "Yes, baby, I will marry you."

Zay released the breath that he was holding and stood up.

"Now that we have gotten that out the way, it's time to finish what I started," he informed me while climbing back into the bed.

Happily, I laid back, accepting all the love that he had to give me.

Gotta Feeling

Zay

.

The next morning while Dionni slept, I got up and went into the living room with the phone at my ear.

"Sash, it's me. Call me back when you get this message." That was the third voicemail that I left on her phone.

After the ordeal that we went through with Candy, I had to be cautious. Something just wasn't right.

At first, I was trying to call Sasha to fill her in on what happened to Candy and my engagement to D.

I knew that she was going to take it bad that Candy may be in jail for a long time, but after hearing that she tried to kill Dionni by hitting her with a car, I think that she would get over it.

I opened my text message screen and texted her. *Call me, it is important.*

That was when I noticed that missed two messages from her. The first text consisted of an 89119 address. I missed that one last night, probably while all that shit was going on with Candy. The second one came through this morning around five.

I stayed with Rain last night. I need you to come get me. I am feeling sick.

She stayed all night with Rain and she's sick? That first message must have be Rain's address. *Ah, she still follows directions*, I thought.

Smiling, I went back into the bedroom and tapped Dionni gently on the shoulder.

"Babe," I said to her when she opened her eyes. "I got to go and get Sasha right now. I missed a couple of calls from her last night and she's not feeling good. Can you please get up and ride with me? I am going to need you to drive my truck back while I drive her car."

Releasing a lazy yawn, she sat up and nodded yes.

"Give me a couple of minutes, baby," she said, sitting up in the bed. "Let me clean myself up and get dressed."

I bent down and kissed her on the forehead. "Thank you, baby," I whispered to her.

She just didn't know how relieved I was. I hadn't spoken to Rain since that night she stood outside my truck watching Dionni and I about to have sex. I had all her calls going straight to voicemail and I ignored all of the text messages.

Maybe if she knew that my fiancée was in the car, she would get the picture and leave me alone.

I went into the bathroom and started the shower.

"Come get into the shower with me so I can help you wake up."

An hour later, we were pulling up to Rain's apartment. I texted her, letting her know I was outside, but I didn't get a response.

"I see her car, but I can't believe Sasha stayed the night here?" Dionni said, shaking her head.

During the ride over, I informed Dionni that Rain was our peeping Tom in the parking garage. I told her everything about relationship, not leaving anything out.

I could tell that she was pissed, but she didn't say anything. I reassured her that everything between Rain and I was over.

I also told her that I wanted her to come with me so that Rain could see that she was only a booty call. Maybe if she seen the two of us together, Rain would get the picture and leave me alone.

Ten minutes went by and still no response from Sasha.

"Baby, let me run upstairs and get her real quick. If I am not out in five minutes, call the police," I told her, getting out the car. I was half way joking, but after all that shit last night with Candy, I was not taking my chances.

"Stay right there while I get into the driver seat. I hate being on this side of town, Zay," she told me. She climbed over the cup holders and got into driver side, rolling down the window.

"I am not playing, Xavier. You got five minutes. What apartment is it? If it takes longer than that, fuck the police. I will be coming to get you myself."

"214," I told her, laughing. I hurried
up the walkway to go find my sister.

Operation

Getting my Man Back

Rain

I was so nervous. Zay was will be here any minute and I was felling giddy. I stood behind the door, wearing only a black lacy bra and matching thong panties.

Knock, Knock, Knock. Startled I jumped and took in a couple of deep breaths.

"He's here," I whispered unlocking the door.

I opened the door and stuck my head out. "Hey Zay, come on in. Sasha is in the bedroom throwing up. "Help me get her."

The moment Zay stepped across the treshhold, it was time for my operation to go into affect. Quickly I tried to close the door behind, swinging the baseball bat that I had behind the door in his direction.

"What the," was all that he could get out of his mouth before I smashed the bat across the back of his head knocking him out cold.

I hurried to grab the tape and pulled his arms behind his back. Zay was bleeding, but I didn't know from where. At this point I had to hurry before he woke up.

I wrapped layers on top of layers of tape around his hands and wrist. I went into the kitchen and grabbed the rope that I purchased this morning from Wal-Mart and tied up his feet.

I rolled him onto his back wiping the sweat off of my face.

Struggling, Zay attempted to open his eyes as I went over to the my small boom box turning on Marvin Gaye's "Let's Get It On."

"Where is my sister," Zay demanded. Your ass is crazy! Bitch!" He exploded struggling to break free.

"Baby, you know that I love you!" I announced straddling him.

"I don't know why you are tripping. Shhh, Mama is gonna help you come to your senses," I cooed taping his mouth shut.

I did not need any of my nosy neighbors fouling up my plan.

"Zay, you are going to be with me if you like it or not. At this point you do not have a choice."

I began to chuckle as I watched him wiggling around underneath me. I stood up swaying my hips to the music.

I wanted to give him a show before we made love thinking that it would loosen him up. But I was wrong. Zay was not paying me any attention.

Dancing my way to the kitchen I picked up the gift that had for him and hid it behind my back.

"Hey, baby," I greeting him walking back slowly and seductively.

I have something for you. I hope you like it."

'Tada," I exclaimed unveiling the twelve long stem roses that I purchased alongside the rope.

"Oh is it not a good time?" I asked him wiping the smile of my face.

The scowl expression that he held showed me that he was not enjoying all my hard work, and he was starting to piss me off.

"I did all this for you baby," told him, this time sitting right on top of his dick. Tenderly, I wiped the blood and sweat from his eyes. I stroked his face, but he winched back in fear.

"I wanted you too see just how much I love you and need you in my life. Why can't you seem to get that through your thick ass skull." I asked, muffing him as I spoke.

I replayed how today was going to be over and over last night. My perception of this moment was different than the scene that was actually taking place.

"So you want me to put your flowers in water?" I asked trying to lighten the mood. I peered around the house in search of a container to put the flowers in.

I got up and retrieved the big gulp cup that I was drinking out of earlier. "Baby, I am so sorry but this is the best that I can do.

I didn't bring anything out here besides me and my clothes." I informed him filling the glass up with water.

"I had to move quickly and get out here to rescue from that bitch Dionni. She doesn't love you like I do. You see Zay, I have been loving you for a long time, and love like that does not just go away over night."

I waited for Zay to respond forgetting that I had his mouth taped up. I needed him to understand that I am the one that he should be with. Not Candy, Dionni, or anyone. Only me.

"Oh I know what I can do to make you feel me. I got another surprise for you baby. I got a bag full of sex toys waiting for us to try out. When we were in Dallas, I didn't get a chance to pull them out.

You left me high and dry Zay, and too do what? To come back to Vegas chasing after another woman Zay? Do you know how you made me feel Zay? DO YOU?"

I was yelling at the top of my lungs. I felt myself becoming madder and madder by the moment. I opened my bag of sex toys and pulled out my .38 caliber that I sometimes had to use to get my point across.

Rocking side to side on top of Zay's chest, I ran the tip of the gun up and down his check and doodled cirles on his face.

I have never seen him look so scared. Zay has always possessed a powerful demeanor. I don't remember ever seeing him flinch. The fear that I felt coming from him turned me on.

"You see Zay, if we are going to have a healthy relationship, I need to start being honest with you.

Remember in Dallas when I told you that my parents stopped paying for my tuition? The didn't stop paying for my tuition, because they never did.

My ex boyfriend Larry was paying for it."

"No, Rain, No." I said interrupting myself. "You just said that you were going to tell the truth, so you need to tell him everything."

Smiling, I nodded to myself, and turned my attention back to Zay.

"I was paying for my tuition with Larry's money. I met Larry on the strip my senior year and fucked the shit out of him, just like I fucked the shit out of you.

Anyway, I followed him to Houston, where I had to convince him that I was all the woman that he needed just like I am going to do with you. He didn't want to hurt his wife's feelings so he told me that I needed to get out.

I didn't want to hurt her but he left me no choice. He cried so badly when I shot her. All of those tears wasted behind that pigeon toed bitch, it was pathetic. We had a small tustle and Larry hit me while trying to escape. I couldn't let him go so easily, so I used the gun that he tried to turn on me, and shot his dumb ass with it."

I don't know why you men don't want me. I am beautiful, powerful in bed, intelligent. I just don't get it. Why don't men like you want to be with me?"

I was so far gone in my tyrade that I wasn't ready for the metal that came across the back of my own head knocking me out cold.

Another one Bites the Dust

Dionni

After ten minutes I began to get restless sitting inside the truck. "What the hell is taking them so long," I said glancing at the time on the dash.

I tried his phone, until I heard the ringing coming from the cup holder. I tried Sasha's phone, but it was going straight to voicemail.

An uneasy feeling swept through my body leaving me with goose bumps up and down my arms.

I didn't want to over react, but afte the stunt Candy pulled last night, I didn't trust none of these crazy ass hoes that Zay has. Six more minutes passed and still no sign of Zay.

Hopping out the car, I pushed the self opening button for his trunk. I was serious when I said I was uncomfortable being over here. I knew what to expect from the hoods that were populized by my "own" people.

The hoods that were populated by everyone else wee the ones that made me uneasy.

Once the trunk door was at full mass, I searched for an item that I could use for protection.

"Damn, my baby is sheltered," I said under my breathe I rummaged through his stuff. There were no tool boxes, work out equipment, nothing inside this brother's trunk.

The only thing that I found that could possibly work was an unsed tire iron. I pushed the button for the trunk to close, slowing walking into the complex.

Thank God, unit 214 was located in the center of the apartments facing what used to be a play ground.

The closer that I got, the more the hairs on the back of my neck stood up. Silently I went up the stairs, steady watching my surroundings. It was still light outside, so the place was like a ghost town.

It wasn't until I was midway up the stairs that I heard a woman's voice screaming. I couldn't make out exactly what she was saying, but by her tone, I could tell that she was pissed.

I pulled my phone out my pocket and called 911. I gave the opearator my location, and told her someone was just shot.

My heart began to race, as I tried to decide what to do. The chick was still ranting, so if I was going to make an entrance, I think now would be the time.

Some of her blinds were missing so I had an opportunity to see what was going on. I got on my hands and knees to and crawling over to the window.

Now if we were in my neighborhood the police would have been here arresting me, but since we were on "Crack Alley," I guess the rules of survival were different.

I seen that Zay was lying on the ground hog tied while some half-naked chick was walking around holding flowers. It wasn't until she turned around that I got a chance to see a glimpse of her face.

It was the same girl that interrupted my love session at the Town Square.

And the plot thickens, I thought to myself shaking my head. I knew that Zay said that he used to sleep with her, but damn, I don't recall him mentioning she was a friend of Sasha's.

"Where the hell was the police," I mumbled under my breath looking down at my phone for the time.

It has only been eight minutes but damn. Look at where we were at. All you seen in this neighborhood were police cruisers, so this was unacceptable.

The girl's voice started to rise again, shaking me out of my thoughts. If I was going to do something, I guess now would be the time.

It wasn't until I stood up, that I realized that there was light shining into the house from the door.

This girl must really be crazy not paying attention that the door wasn't closed all the way. I held the tire iron close to my body as I peered inside the door. The girl was now perched ontop of Zay having a full conversation, answering herself and everything.

It was now or never, I thought to myself as I squeezed through the crack.

Sasha was no where in sight as I crept closer to the pair. Neither one of them noticed me, but it wasn't until I got directly behind her that I could what was hold their attention.

She was running a gun up and down Zay's chest. Asking him why she could't find a man that wanted to be with her.

I lifted the iron above my head and swinging the metal at her with all my might. Blood went flying every where.

I pushed her off of Zay, kicking the gun away. Gently I pulled the tape of his mouth and kissed his lips.

"Help me sit up please baby," he asked struggling to get up. I helped him and hurried into the kitchen grabbing a knife.

"Baby, I haven't seen Sasha the entire time that I have been here," he informed me, as I cut tape from around his hand.

Once he was free, I handed him the

knife so he could remove the rope, and picked back up my faithful tire iron in search for Sasha.

The apartment wasn't that big, but this chick has clearly proven her point that she was crazy. Who knows what she had behind door number one and two.

I opened the first room door slowly and peered inside. The only thing there was an air mattress and clothes all over the floor.

I could hear my heart beating in my ears, as I pushed open door number two. I let out a sigh of relief when I laid eyes on Sasha, who was lying on the floor; hands, feet, and mouth tied up just like her brother.

"Baby, she's in here," I yelled helping her up. Her face was tear stained and her mane was all over the place.

Removing the tape from her mouth she let out a loud cry, coughing at the same time. Once Zay stepped into the room, the sounds of sirens could be heard outside.

He scooped Sasha into his arms, spreading kisses throughout her face. Quickly he removed her restraints and picked her up into arms carrying her out of the room.

Chuckling under his breath, Zay turned his attention to me.

"Baby, thank you for saving the day and all, but I thought we agreed that you were only going to wait five minutes before you called the police. Hell, it's been over an hour, and they are just getting here. What kind of hero are you?" he asked shaking his head.

"The kind that loves your yellow butt," I retorted placing my hands on my hips. Love is the only thing that is going to allow me to marry you after all this. You better let the rest of your groupies know that I am not the one to have twisted."

Epilogue

Tiana

Even though I had to end up in the hospital for Dionni to come home, I am just glad that she did.

Dionni finally let down her wall so that she can obtain some sort of closure when it came to her relationship with Dale. The two of them sat down and talked and I can honestly say now, they are on a road to recovery.

Dionni was going to marry Zay; while Dale and Ashley were trying to work on a real *relationship*.

Eva and Dionni were taking baby steps. They have starting to talk more and they even went shopping together.

I had to give it to Candy. She spent a week in captivitiy and like a thief in the night, she disappeared. She moved back to L. A. vowing to herself that she was going to make the most out of life due to the second chance that she was given.

Even though Rain as in prison for attempted murder, I felt sorry for her. She was settling down on D block within the walls of Smiley Lane; a woman's correctional facility in Las Vegas instead of a mental institution where I felt that she belonged.

Dale and Ashley asked Twan and I to be Raven's God mother. When I was in the hospital, the doctor informed me that there may not be a chance for me to become a mother. Due to the scarring that

I received during the rape.

As for me. Antwan and I were taking it one day at a time. I felt myself getting stronger and stronger everyday. We had a long road to go. But I had faith that we could get through it.

God worked everything out in his favor. I think my ordeal made all of us grow individually. It allowed us to see that life is too short. We have to accept the good with the bad and move on.

Twisted

Its crazy,

You would think

That having everything

Come out in the open

Would make me feel

A sigh of relief

Forces me to come

Up with an ultimatum

But the distance

Between us

Seem to have

Brought us closer

I was sure

That finding out about

Your secret life

Would have stayed away

But I guess like they say

Opposites do attract

Because it only

Taken us to

A height that only u and I
Could reach

But the words

That you express

Does not make me feel
That we finally can begin,

It feels that we still

Have major road
Blocks that still lie ahead

On a twisted path

I can take this ride

With you

But only for so long

However words are not enough

Actions must take place

You may think
We have time

But as time goes

So does my worth.

It hurts me to say we

need a break

and take time to think.

I love you

past our desires

and when we talk

it feels that our souls

become erect and strong

entwining just to
touch each other

even though we have

been far apart.

Understand where I am

coming from when I say

You're what I want

But I also deserve more

And I want you

To be with me.

I am officially

pouring my heart to you

You got me Twisted.......

Ni'cola

Acknowledgements

First I would like to give honor to God, through whom all things are possible. I would like to thank you for wrapping your arms around me and keeping me sane. A lot of things happened to me during the course of writing this book, but I can honestly say that it wasn't for my Belief in steadfast Faith, I never would have made it.

Destani and Diamond, I am so proud of you. You both have grown into mature and beautiful young ladies, and I thank you for holding me down every day. I love you☺

To my family the Mitchell, Taylor, LeFear, Hicks, Smith clans, thanks so much for all of your support. We have been through so much this past year by losing our backbone, but I know that she is smiling down on all of us. Her main goal in life was to keep up together, and I can honestly say, we are doing a good job loving and relying on one another. I love you all so much.

To my staff at NCM Publishing: We got another one under our belt. Thank you for believing in me, and dealing with me. This is our year. I can feel it!

Leila Jefferson…. You are my backbone. Without you, none of these novels would be in existence. I love you for dealing with my ADHD tail and understand the method behind my madness.

To the authors on the roster of NCM: Imani True, Dreama Skye, Rekaya Gibson, and Patricia Bridewell. You ladies are beautiful and I want to thank you as well for dealing with me. I love you all from the bottom of my heart. I hope you know that.

Ms. ROCURLINC herself….Greetings..… lol Thank you for taking my projects and running with them . You have had my back since day one and I love that. You are the true definition of pit bull in a skirt. I love you girlie. Really I do.

To my prized possessions Joey Pinkney, Tamika Newhouse, and QB Wells…. Joey, thank you for believing in me. World let me tell you, when I met him I couldn't stand him, but now, I can't see a day go past, and I go on without him..I love you with all of my heart. Ms. New New…You know I would be lost if I couldn't call you my literary sistah. We have been through some ish… and you know it still more to come. I love you girl. Professor… Thank you for putting me onto so much game. Thank you for believing in me. You know I love you too boo.

Ms. Ronna BABY, you made this cover come to life! You are such a beautiful person. Thank you for loving and believing in me. I am blessed to have *you* in my corner being protective of me and my girls. LOL. Real talk, Destani looks up to you. Thank you for being such a positive role model. Dionni's back yell, I don't think that you're ready...

Mz. Haute Thrifture, Mik So Chic Thank you listening to my vision and bring it to life. You made something as simple as a pair of jeans and big earrings into a work of art. I am so proud of you girl. Live your dreams baby. Make that ish a reality.

KayBee... you are a true artist! You know how to capture that shot and running with it. You are such a beast on the graphics. The world is not ready! I love being asked, "is that shirt that has twisted on it for sale?" When I tell them that you tattooed that on her, no one believes me.. You are the best.

Steeve... my friend, and my hype man. You have been my best friend ever since I came here, and I thank you for never stop loving me. Thank you for the constant push, love, and support.

To my Literary Family.... Jessica Robinson, Michael Lewis, Tina McKinney, Eric Deloach, Avah LeReaux, Theresa Gonsalves, Michele Fletcher, Sistar Tea, Loretta R. Walls, Pittershawn Palmer, J M Benjamin, K'Wan, Chris Hicks, Toshia Shaw, Corey Barnes, LaQuita Adams, George Hudson, Jazz Ma Taz, Peron Long, Queen BG. I love all of you. Every year, you stand by me, even when I go into hiding. This year has been tough for me with the loss of my sister, but all of you stood by me. Thank you!

Meet the Author

Striving to establish a new flair to the term contemporary fiction, Best-Selling author Ni'cola Mitchell entered the literary scene with one main objective: *To Stimulate Your Mind, One Word at a Time.*

Through her independent publishing company NCM Publishing; Ni'cola published her debut novel entitled *Over and Over Again* in June 2009. Following on the heels of her debut's critical acclaim, *The Appetizer: When You're Not His Main Course* was released February 2010. Ni'cola's growing readership eagerly awaits her next literary masterpiece *Twisted*, due out December 2010. Much of her work revolves around complex relationship issues situations and Mitchell's compulsive desire to see women over come challenges.

Over and Over Again was featured in the top ten by EDC Creations Recommended Reading List for the 2009 fall season under Mainstream Fiction and Women's Fiction. She was recently nominated Self-Published Author of the Year with the African-African Literary Awards Show. She is also a member of the national touring group the Literary Sistah's.

Because of her outstanding representation of Las Vegas' African-American community, she was featured in the second edition of Who's Who in Black Las Vegas. Ni'cola is also a motivational speaker and literary consultant. When Ni'cola isn't writing, she loves to spend time with her family and volunteer as a mentor for youth activities.

Originally from Kingston, Jamaica, Ni'cola Mitchell currently resides in North Las Vegas, Nevada, with her two daughters, Destani and Diamond. She holds a Bachelors degree of Science in Business Management and is currently pursuing a Masters of Business Administration in HealthCare Management.

Find out more at www.nicolacmitchell.com

Also From the Pen of

Ni'cola

An Excerpt from

Candy

Due out Spring Time 2012

www.ncmpublishing.com

Candy

"Mommy!" I screamed as I jumped up out of my sleep. My gown was drenched in sweat and my heart was racing. I opened my eyes as the tears escaped rolled down my cheeks.

I tried to regain my composure and took in a couple of deep breathes. No matter what I did, those tragic flashbacks fought to stay in existence in my mind.

My memories continued to win the battle of making me relive that horrible night.

The night of my thirteenth birthday; when I lost my Momma and my innocence.

I could still see my Momma's face and smell his horrific breath.

Eric, my Momma's boyfriend was the cause of my pain and constant grief.....

NCM PUBLISHING PRESENTS

NCM PUBLISHING PRESENTS

MAMA DON'T LIKE

UGLY

REKAYA GIBSON

NCM PUBLISHING PRESENTS

Strawberries
Stilettos
&
Steam

EROTIC TALES BY IMANI TRUE AND DREAMA SKYE

Visit www.ncmpublishing.com to view all of our titles.